Awaydays

KEVIN SAMPSON

JONATHAN CAPE
LONDON

Published by Jonathan Cape 1998

2 4 6 8 10 9 7 5 3 1

Copyright © Kevin Sampson 1998

Kevin Sampson has asserted his right
under the Copyright Designs and Patents Act 1988
to be identified as the author of this work

First published in Great Britain in 1998 by
Jonathan Cape
Random House, 20 Vauxhall Bridge Road,
London SW1V 2SA

Random House Australia (Pty) Limited
20 Alfred Street, Milsons Point, Sydney,
New South Wales 2061, Australia

Random House New Zealand Limited
18 Poland Road, Glenfield,
Auckland 10, New Zealand

Random House South Africa (Pty) Limited
Endulini, 5A Jubilee Road, Parktown 2193, South Africa

Random House UK Limited Reg. No. 954009
A CIP catalogue record for this book is available from the British Library

ISBN 0–224–05055–9

Papers used by Random House UK Limited are natural,
recyclable products made from wood grown in sustainable forests.
The manufacturing processes conform to the environmental
regulations of the country of origin.

Typeset by Deltatype Ltd, Birkenhead, Merseyside
Printed and bound in Great Britain by
Mackays of Chatham PLC

18 November 1979

You can always tell how good your mob's going to be by the amount of young ones who turn up. Judging by the contingent of Juniors gathered outside The Tub's off-licence, aggressively smoking Number Six and flicking baby fringes out of their eyes, we're going to have a fuck of a good crew today. I let on to Billy Powell and a couple of the other little urchins and head on inside The Dock public house, Ilchester Square, Birkenhead, locally known as The Bloodtub, there to meet with the esteemed gentlemen of The Pack.

The Pack are Tranmere Rovers' away crew and a splendid bunch they are, too. Today I shall be joining them in an excursion to Wrexham for one of the biggest dates in the footballing calendar. Today is the First Round Proper of the F.A. Cup, a time for every ramshackle club from Hartlepool to Exeter to start harbouring dreams of brief encounters with the giants of soccer. Hereford against Newcastle. Colchester against Leeds. Every year the Cup throws up an unlikely combination and every year one of the underdogs forces an upset. Who knows what might happen if we got drawn against Tottenham or Villa or someone? Certain mayhem.

But let's not get too misty-eyed about the Romance of the Cup. While most of us can work up an impressive frenzy for a scrambled equaliser at Rochdale, we don't follow Tranmere for their progressive, free-flowing football. Our satisfaction comes from earning our rep as the nastiest little crew in the Third, and for us the magic of the F.A. Cup is that it never fails to deliver the ag. The First Round in particular *always* means trouble. Whether it's Hyde United or Leek Town, everyone's mobbed up for the Cup.

Even Wrexham. I've seldom known a game so eagerly anticipated as this local spat with despised woollyback foes, Wrexham. They hate us with the proper, decent, resentful fury of a serf who loathes his oppressor, but we just hold them in contempt as an underclass – a Birmo-wearing, feather-barnetted sub-species who pronounce the 'W' in their name when they're trying to leg you. It can be hairy, sometimes, being outnumbered by hordes of inbreds in places like Mansfield, but there's nothing more calming than hearing them speak. There's no way you can be hurt by someone who calls you '*youth*', and when Wrexham come charging at you, arms stretched out as wide as they'll go, screaming '*Wuh-reck-sem*' at full, red-faced force, you know you're going to have a laugh. We thought we'd lost them for good when they gained promotion last season, leaving us with only Chester and Crewe for local grudge games. But here we are. Back again to torment them. There's going to be murder. So it's worth the excursion to Birkenhead North just to meet up with the crew, even though I could've just got on at Neston. None of them really know where I live, other than it's out of town – not even Elvis – but I could've easy made up an excuse for jumping on there. But that's not the point – not all of it, anyway. You want to be there, in the thick, from the off.

It's just gone eleven when I step into The Tub, but some of the heads look like they've been here hours. Surveying the pub I immediately feel a rush of pride – this mob'd give anyone a run for their money. Marty O'Connor, shaven ginger bullet-head nodding to The Stranglers on the jukey. Baby Millan, fresh-faced Stanley merchant, joking with a couple of Saturday girls from Park Hampers. Eddie Spark and John Godden arguing with Batesy about Secret Affair and The Glory Boys. Elvis, shockingly thin, greets me with his irony-laden grin, eyes screwed up, looking like a technicolor Bryan

Ferry in his livid purple box leather. Flicking and blowing at his monstrous plum-dyed wedge, Elvis beckons me to the bar.

'A'right, Carty. State of Batesy rowing about the fucken Mods. Even fucken Wrexham are wearing parkas these days. Fucken beauts.'

Elvis and I are perhaps the most fashion-obsessed of The Pack, which is a pretty fucking well-dressed crew by anybody's standards. Most of us have wedges or side-partings and wear Samba or Stan Smith trainies, Lois jeans and cardigans. One or two of the older lads have still got BeeGee centre-parts and sheepies, but that's expected of blokes in their twenties. They like to take the piss out of us lot freezing to death in rainlashed away ends, but they've seen the way the girls flock around us wherever we go. We look the part, and everyone knows it. One time, Marty O'Connor brought a can of blue spray paint to the match and offered to spray our lips and fingers blue.

'What's the fucken problem?' he cackled, when we all started running from the drifting aerosol jet. 'It's Adidas paint. For that latest Odgie frozen look!'

Odgie. Marty favours the New Skin look. One minute Slaughter And The Dogs were asking where all the Boot Boys went, next thing we've got Sham 69 and a new breed of skinheads. It's pretty big with the diehard mob from the North End who still see Birkenhead as an old dockers' community. This crew *hate* Scousers, a prejudice not weakened by the latest bouts of trouble between Liverpool and Tranmere. It's doing everyone's swedes in that the Scousers still see us as Wools, no matter that we dress the same as them. Marty and Eddie Spark and a lot of the older lads can't understand why we want to look like Odgies. They'd prefer us all to be boneheads. I don't mind a few skins in The Pack, they always look evil, but our whole identity, the whole point of The Pack and the reason we've got this rep, is that we look and behave like no one else in this Division.

They haven't got a clue in the Third. Liverpool started the

wedgehead look last season and, with us being so nearby, Tranmere soon had our own little mob. There's only really Stockport and Fulham who are on the case and even with them it's only a dozen, twenty boys at the most. But it's the ultimate going to places like Chesterfield dressed like this. They're a race apart. They clock the haircuts and they're straight on to us. The ritual never varies. There's always loads of them, tattooed up and shitters to a man. They wait outside the station and when we get off the train, about sixty of us, no noise, no scarves, they start walking round the forecourt with their hands on their hips, making these sort of girlie whooping noises. They really think that because we haven't got borstal tatts and three scarves each that we're going to be easy. And that we'll be cross that they don't like our gear. It's maximum joy, every time when we run in and pure give it to them. Their faces are too much. They do not know what is going on, and when the blades come out . . . well, they're older and wiser by the time the sun sets. Tranmere are the only crew in the Third who go away by train and we're the only ones who use Stanleys – as Chesterfield and all the other knobheads now know.

'Make 'em leave 'em behind!'

'You what?'

'Serious. Make 'em take 'em off and leave 'em behind the bar. Can't be going to Wrexham with fucken parkas on board. Make a holy fucken show of us.'

Elvis laughs.

'You tell 'em!'

We just get halves at Elvis' behest and stop by Batesy's table to josh him about his attire.

'Come 'ead, Batesy! Let's see it!'

'You wha'?'

'Come on, open wide!'

4

I lunge for his mouth. Batesy recoils.

'Koff, you beaut! Fuck's goin' on?'

Elvis is doubled up, laughing. I put one arm around Batesy and grip his lower lip with my thumb and forefinger.

'Come 'ead! We just wanna see your tatt! Where is it? M-O-D, isn't it? Fuckenell, Batesy, thought you was meant to be the Ace Face!'

Batesy grins. For all that he's a bit of a dullard he's got respect, he's a ferocious fighter and it's only lately that I've felt entitled to join in the piss-taking – not just with him, but generally. Batesy's in good spirits and tells us that some of the Legends, Casey and Ally Quinn and some of the older Woodchurch heads are considering coming out of retirement for this one, such is the lure of the Cup. Batesy's lack of guile is in no way disguised by his various speech impediments. Although he has the stutter pretty much under control, he can't distinguish between *th*, *v* and *f* sounds, and, worse, has a babyish inability to pronounce his *r* sounds. Thus did Port Fale wun like wabbits outside the Ficky Lodge back in August.

It transpires that The Tub has been open all night and Batesy launches into a highly involved and highly unlikely-sounding tale casting himself and Ally Quinn as tireless Lotharios in a twos-up with Toothless Elsa, one of The Tub's glamorous barmaids. We all laugh raucously, neither believing Batesy's tale nor caring whether it's true. There's a brilliant atmos. Everyone knows it. Today is going to be an epic.

Me and Elvis stand by the door sipping our halves, watching all the little ones congregate outside the station. They look smart, miniature scals in cords, trainies and Adidas windcheaters. There's some good little ruckers there. Billy Powell's only about fourteen but he's been very useful on more than one occasion. Most of the Junior Squad – mainly the rats from the Ford and the Woodchurch – will get on at Upton. So with the firm we've already got here and allowing for a few to get on at Bidston, we're looking good for a crew of eighty-plus on the ten past twelve which should well be enough to do Wrexham – even on F.A. Cup day.

Already on board the train is Damien O'Connor, Marty's kid brother. He's walking up and down the coaches with an empty sweet jar, cadging bits of drink off the older lads for his now-traditional Pack Punch. So far in the jar he's got Carlsberg Special Brew, Bacardi, vodka, Scotch and, lending the concoction a thick, sickly density, a full can of Coke.

'Any contributions, gents?'

'You lot should lay off the ale,' says Elvis.

He's a fucking downer when he's like this, Elvis. When he feels like drinking it's cool, Jim Morrison liked a drink, name me one great artist – *great* – artist who didn't benefit from some form of consciousness-enhancing stimulus, blah, blah, blah. But when he's off the plonk, all boozers are subbies, makes you sluggish, blunts your instinct for danger, etc etc etc. This common sense, incidentally, coming from the first boy I ever saw cut somebody, temple to top lip, with a Stanley craft knife. He's a loony, Elvis, but that's all part of his appeal.

'You'll be fucken useless by Wrexham.'

He might well say that, but some of us actually *need* a drink before games like this. The butterflies are already jumping and we're only just past Bidston. Elvis stands up, scrawny and completely arse-free even in the snuggest of Lois and delves inside his jacket.

'In fact . . .'

He pulls out a little paper wrap. I notice a drop of blood on his finger tip where he's nicked himself. I keep telling him to retract the blade when he's carrying – it causes havoc with the lining of your jacket. He unwraps the whizz.

'C'mere.'

Damien holds out the sweet jar while Elvis carefully tips half the wrap of pinkish powder into the vicious black mix. He whips out his Stanley and, much to the amusement of

6

everyone around us, stirs the liquid to a frothy foment and hands it back to little Damien.

'If you're going to be mad you may as well know what you're doing.'

Damien grins and slopes away to the corner of the coach, where he tries to wedge himself in firmly enough to get a good slug of punch without the jolting of the train sending it all over him. He smacks his lips and winces comically. Elvis passes me the speed. I avoid the bloody bit where his cut finger's been dabbing.

'D'you see the *Whistle Test?*'

'Nar. Fucken fell asleep in me chair, waiting.'

Elvis leans forward, eyes alive with his own special madness.

'Ah, I can't believe you missed it, man. Joy Division. Completely out there. Curtis, man ...'

I nod my understanding, even though I didn't see this latest performance. Elvis and I saw Joy Division playing an Amnesty benefit at Eric's back in May. We'd mainly gone to see Kleenex and The Raincoats, all-girl bands who, Trots or not, might have been pleased to know that their record sleeves provided wanking fodder for many a lonely adolescent. But it was Joy Division who blew us away. Ian Curtis threw so much angst and demented energy into his show that he collapsed after four or five songs. They couldn't have been on stage more than half an hour, but it was completely stunning. And they just kept getting better. Just a couple of months ago we went to the Futurama in Leeds and, out of a line-up which included Soft Cell, The Human League, Echo And The Bunnymen and U2, it was Joy Division that slayed us. Elvis and I often talk about a suicide pact played out to 'New Dawn Fades'.

Everyone cranes forward as the train pulls in at Upton, hoping for a good crew to supplement the fine mob already on board. Some sight awaits us. It's not just the usual urchins and robbers we were expecting, who're pushing forward on the

7

platform, but a full-scale crew of Woody, too. There's some real heads there, Hardy, Kev The Man, Christy Byatt in a green beret, all pogoing madly and twatting each other with rolled-up newspapers. Hardy's wearing an eyepatch, which looks sound, even though there's fuck all wrong with his minces far as I know. And there's a lad with a crutch, putting on a bit of a limp. A crutch or a couple of arms in slings always looks boss mixed up in the main body of the crew. I reckon that there's easy thirty of them, a comical sight next to the handful of silent ice-skaters who'll get off at Shotton for Deeside Leisure Centre. I push my way to the window for a better look and am immediately taken over by a woozy affection for the vast redbrick tower blocks of the Ford Estate on one side of the tracks and the stark white blocks of the Woodchurch on the other. Not for the first time do I find my butterflies replaced by a heady euphoria. I grab Damien.

'Give us a go on that before these twats get on.'

I take a slug of Damien's magic potion and lick my lips. I know that something's going to happen today and I know that I'm going to be right in there. More often than not I'll just go with the flow at aways, doing the minimum expected. I never run, obviously, but I'm not one for sticking my neck out too much, either. It's to do with protocol. There are people like Marty and John Godden who you look to to start the rows and, while there are times when you think they might be dragging their heels a bit, they're the Boys. It's up to them. I'm ever conscious of the fact that this is only the start of my third season with The Pack and I'm only just getting to be accepted. Sometimes, though, I can't help myself, I get this headrush, this mad adrenalin surge just comes over me, a delirious, fierce, loyal pride in The Pack. I feel like I'd do anything for them.

I can feel it now as the train jerks to a halt and I lick the residue grains of sulphate from my teeth. I'm going to make sure that everyone knows who I am today, not least these Woodchurch names getting on now. I nod to individuals I know to let on to, but who aren't regulars. The fantasy of the Cup and the fact that it's Wrexham has brought all kinds out. It's one hell of a crew, and I belong right here with the best of them.

Two lads we know from Eric's and the tunnel bus come and stand by Elvis and me. When I say we know them, all we ever say to each other is 'A'right'. Don't even know their names. We always call them The Spics, because they look a tad Latino. *Portuguese*, Elvis decided one night after too much homegrown at a Cabaret Voltaire gig. That was about the last time we really tried to talk to them. They're not actively unfriendly, just silent – and quite psychotic in an off. Danny Allen, a Scouse lad who came to live on the Nocky last summer, comes and joins the company.

'A'right, Paul.' He always calls me by my proper name, Danny, probably on account of having had to come into the office on official business one time. It's only a job to me, but it spooks the public. They think they'll never get out alive.

'Howdy, Danny. Cracker mob, eh?'

'Too fucken right, lad. These'd see off Liverpool, these would.'

He's always a bit wary about being from Liverpool and, since all the trouble started again, over-compensates by running the Odgies down at any opportunity. He's alright, though. Bit of a shithouse. I tried to get everyone calling him Danny Jekyll – he was always hiding – but it never caught on.

'Want to watch it at Buckley,' warns Danny. 'Went to Wrexham with the other lot in the League Cup last year.' He pulls a face which would seem to indicate that Buckley is not far shy of The Bowery in the naughty neighbourhood stakes. 'Buckley, lar. Tell you. Ambush City. Smashed every window on the fucken train.'

Like we don't know about Buckley.

'I tell you, Danny, if there's one cunt at Buckley who wants to fucken know we're off this fucken train. No messing about.'

9

Disappointingly, there's no reception committee at Buckley. As our train pulls off again, two lads emerge from the shelter giving it 'wanker' signs. They're pure Wrexham shite, these two, the sort who'll jump on your head when it's six-onto-one. I heave down the window and start shouting at the nearest and bigger of the two. Buck teeth. Scuzzy little bumfluff moustache. Laughable attempt at dressing like us. What did he think? We were going to start respecting Wrexham for trying to dress the part? See them in a new light? What a complete cunt he looks. Shit Harrington, shit, nondescript Wrangler drainies, shit, dirty Green Flash. Utterly shit attempt at a wedge, obviously done by his big sister from a drawing. Elvis and I have a hoot about this, Elvis doing his Ifor The Engine voice.

'*Knorrr*, sis, it's, like, *long* on one side and sort of, *short* on the other.'

'Like him out of Human League, yeah?'

'Yeoman League?'

Batesy comes around, as he does every single away game, counting up how many there is on the train. There's a bit of a dispute in the next carriage. We've just passed Gwersyllt and John Godden is trying to get everyone off at the next stop, Wrexham General. Wrexham General is on the outskirts of town, but close to Wrexham's ground. Marty and Eddie want to stay on until Wrexham Central and have a good mosie round the town, see what's happening. It's not even one o'clock yet, and Marty wants to know what the fuck we're going to do for two hours on this side of Wrexham. Godden reckons he's had a tip-off.

'They'll be there, la. In The Turf. Fucken hundreds of the cunts.'

'Wrexham haven't *got* fucken hundreds.'

'I'm telling you. Ally's cousin works at Marshall's. They're bang up for this one. If you think it's going to be a doddle, you can fucken think again.'

'Sound. I hope there *is* hundreds of them. They'll need every one.'

'Let's just get off next stop. If they're there, we have it with them. If not, we walk back into town. It's only half a fucken mile.'

'And what if they're all there at Central, waiting for us and we don't turn up? Do we want them going round saying we bottled it?'

'Fuck off, Marty! We'll fucken cane them wherever they are! And you *know* where they are.'

'Yeah. Maybe. But I fancy getting myself a new jacket, first. There's not many shops by the ground, is there?'

Godden looks like he's going to spark Marty, then he breaks into a broad smile.

'Why didn't you just say?'

'I like winding you up, you cunt.'

Danny Allen decides that this is the moment for him to step in, the voice of reason.

'Let's just go into Wrexham fucken town or whatever and sniff out their boys. There's bound to be *some* cunt there, eh?'

Like he'll be leading the charge. Batesy tries one last argument for getting off next stop and is laughed down.

'Batesy's going to take the old men's Social Club on his todd,' laughs Elvis. 'Make sure you twat that cunt Geraint Williams! Old Geraint! Mad bastard!'

No one's sure what Elvis is on about, but we laugh raucously anyway. Batesy is held down as we pull into Wrexham General and only allowed up after his head has been peppered with knuckles. Everyone seems pretty intent on ragging the town come what may, and there's a huge roar as the antiquated two-car train finally comes to a standstill at Wrexham Central.

'Let's! Give! De Wrexham!' shouts Godden, booting the carriage door open.

'A LIRRUL BIRRA KNUCKLE!!' scream the mob.

11

Everyone pours off the train, chanting and wilding down the platform and out into the streets. We stop for a brief moment, unsure where to go first, then the mob starts splitting up and going in different directions.

The Juniors, who are too diminutive to even think about getting served, go off on the rob. They'll be a cracker little firm when they're older, these. They're scared of nothing and really look after each other. Most of the crew who got on at Upton go off for a mooch, which leaves the regular Pack, plus Christy, Hardy and Kev from Woodchurch, to go looking for Wrexham's finest. A trek around the small pedestrianised centre yields a cruddy Lord Anthony bubble jacket for Marty, who thinks it's smart, along with a few dirty looks from disgruntled shoppers. No Wrexham, though. An over-friendly Busy comes over to make our acquaintance with his sour-faced female accomplice in tow.

'Hello there, boys. Not going to cause us any problems today, are you?'

'Not if your shithouse boyos keep hiding from us, we won't.'

The Busy tries to keep things light, saying he's on for a shag if he gets home early today, but the WPC is in no mood for conspiring with scum like us. She warns us and moves us on. Up ahead there's a gang of kids shouting and lobbing bottles, but even if we could be arsed, which we can't, they'd just leg it before we got within twenty yards of them. Leave them to the Juniors. Half a dozen of them'd turn those pricks over.

'This is shite!' says Godden. 'The fucken F.A. Cup! I've been looking forward to this for weeks! I fucken told you where they'd be! Let's fucken get down the ground and get into these twats!'

'Ah, fuck it!' says Marty, pulling up outside a ropey-looking pub called The Mitre. 'Let's have a bevvy in here. Come 'ead! We've done enough fucken walking . . .'

Danny Allen convinces Godden that Wrexham's crew drink

in The Mitre during midweek. We troop inside. The place is deserted. Somehow the energy and excitement of before is being sapped by all the bickering and aimless wandering about. Godden's right. We should just get down to the ground and see what's what. There's no way that Wrexham are not going to show. Of course they'll be there. They're a bigger club than us, now, starting to sell themselves as the Welsh Nationalist team and attract support from all over North Wales. Bloody Wales play their home games at The Racecourse, these days. This is the F.A. Cup. They'll be there. Elvis and I stand dixie on the door while Kev The Man empties the fruit-machine with snide ten-bobs.

There's a roar from outside in the streets nearby and, as the three of us try to get out of the door all at once to see who's coming, a crew of thirty-odd swarms over the wire fencing at the back of the train station. Elvis runs back inside the pub, near hysterical.

'COME 'EAD!!' How many legendary skirmishes have been started with those two simple words? Elvis is almost unrecognisable.

'Come 'ead!! They're here! They're fucken having a go!'

Everyone's on their feet and out of the pub, glasses in hand, ready to have it. There's the usual shouts of 'Stand!' as we lose our shape at the sides, too many trying to run in all at once. I can barely breathe. My eyes are darting everywhere, trying to pick a target, hoping to find Bucktooth, the standoff.

He's nowhere to be seen. What I see is vaguely familiar faces. Hardy and Kev are laughing and doubling over on their knees, breathless. This mob we've been fronting are all older lads, late twenties and thirties, mainly Woodchurch heads who used to go to Tranmere years ago. Shit. The Legends are here. Now it *is* going to be a doddle.

We all have a good laugh about the near-battle and decide to walk to the ground. Marty seems happier. The incident has taken away a lot of the tension and The Legends keep the good humour going with a barrage of sly jokes aimed at a fat skin in their midst, Billy Money. Casey revels in the story about how they all went to Southport in the Sixties, when Southport were in the League, and a load of Skem boys surrounded them at the fair. Billy Money loudly and visibly shit his Skinners, an incident he's still gamely living down and attributing to a bad pint. Up ahead some of the Junior Squad are legging it back from the direction of the ground, faces contorted. Damien, frenzied with hooch and speed, can barely get his words out.

'There's about a thousand of them down there! They're giving it to us bad style, man! Axes and everything!'

Elvis and I glance at Godden, who shrugs and smirks. He's been right all along, but in a way so's Marty. What if Wrexham *had* been waiting at the station? We've probably done things right, after all. Danny Allen gulps.

'A fucken thousand! Where'd all them come from!'

Elvis laughs.

'You know what a Junior Squad thousand is, la. Twenty skinheads and a gang of Mods. Come 'ead!'

Christy and Casey and Quinny and all the Woody crew have already started breaking up fences and kicking over buckling walls for bricks. Christy picks up a brick in each hand.

'COME 'EAD!!' he screams, charging ahead of The Pack, pop-eyed. There's a tremendous roar from our over-confident mob and we pile forward, keen to get into this mythical Wrexham firm. Again I catch John Godden's eye, waiting for him and Marty to give the okay, but he's struggling to be heard above the fracas and everyone is running past, screaming and hurling masonry.

There's a dip in the road by General station, more of a hump than a bridge, but down below there's a huge mob of Wrexham walking back towards The Turf. For a second Christy stops and everyone hesitates. Wrexham's tail end turn round, startled by the furore, and instinctively back off. Marty and John come pushing out of the thick of The Pack, take one look at Wrexham and go tanking down the slope into the middle of them. It's like Rob Roy. Everyone's into them double-fast, no exceptions. Most of their boys just turn and run, but there's still a good mob ready to stand toe-to-toe and get stuck in. I bang a lad under the nose and his top lip just bursts, blood and snot everywhere and he's down, snivelling.

'Come 'ead Tranmere, these are shite!' yells Hardy, smacking a Mod repeatedly with what looks like a cosh, still whacking him when he's out cold, gaping like a cod. The lad with the limp wades in, lashing out with his crutch. The purple of Elvis catches my eye. There's two Wrexham on him, one on his back trying to pull him down while his mate slips trying to kick Elvis in the balls. Another lad runs over with a big wooden stave above his head, a whole fencepole, ready to brain Elvis. Before I can get to him he brings the thing crashing down but Elvis swerves away and, in one movement, spins and slashes the lad behind him on the back of his hand. The one on the floor tries to crawl away but I volley him in the guts with my left and give him a beauty on the side of his ear. The hero with the stave stands rooted to the spot, staring at Elvis's blade like it won't get him if he keeps his eye on it. Elvis bounces over and stripes him on the top of his scalp and jumps back, crouched low in front of the poor cunt, ready to give him more. A thin trickle of blood runs quickly down his forehead, splitting into a fork around his nose and down his bloated cheeks. Still he grips his stave. I jump in and boot him in the side, this time making him drop the wood, and Elvis goes again, his familiar jerky action savaging the wool. He goes down and Elvis seems happy to leave it, but I've got to finish the cunt off. He looks up at me stupidly and tries to say something, so I pick up his lump of wood and crack him with it. He curls up in a ball to protect himself and I feel his knuckles pop as I twat his hands with the stave.

Blade terror has gone through them – they're convinced

that every one of us is tooled up – and they start to back away towards the ground without actually turning and fleeing. There's only about five or six regular Stanley merchants in The Pack, plus a couple of hammers and coshes, but it's obvious that Wrexham will try and play on this and use it as an excuse. I feel a bit of anti-climax because I know we still would've gone through them today, without the hardware and without Casey and Co.

More police arrive on horseback and with snarling dogs. Some of the older Wrexham skins are mobbing up again outside The Turf, trying to get their crew to stand. The dog handlers drive them back against the turnstiles and pen them in, while the horses try to scatter Tranmere down towards our end. It's just shouting and barking, as we try to push back against the plod while keeping away from those slobbering hounds. Old Bill is succeeding, slowly, in heaving us back away from the Wrexham end when another train pulls in at Wrexham General. It's full of Tranmere quilts, but their sheer volume pushing out of the station helps to break the police cordon. A big shout, and we charge back towards the Wrexham end, but by now they're inside the ground, hanging over the sides gobbing on us and throwing missiles. Kids in the road are crying at the relentless barking of the alsatians and the glass smashing at their feet as their dads try to steer a path through us lot, with bottles and halfies raining down from the Wrexham end.

'Feckin' shit, Tranmere!'

I knew it.

'Feckin' nethin' without your blades! Shithouses!'

We surge back at the gates. The Busies lose patience and run the dogs right into the middle of us, scattering us across the road.

'Stand, Tranmere! Fucken stand!' shouts Batesy, a cut eyelid flickering manically. 'Do the fucken dogs if you have to!!' This causes so much mirth in the ranks that any lingering hopes of a proper assault on the gates vanish there and then. Do the dogs!

We win the match 1–0 and could've scored more, sparking scenes of delirium among the trainspotters and providing the unfamiliar situation of still being in the draw for the next round of the Cup. The Busies keep us in for half an hour after the game. It crosses my mind that if we're half the crew we think we are, we ought to be able to turn over a few hick Busies and smash our way out of the ground. Looking round, though, I can see that everyone's heads have dropped. The older boys, who've been drinking, are just fucked and want to go home and the plod give us such a heavy escort to Wrexham General that even Marty abandons plans to go drinking in the town after the game. There's a prevailing feeling of depression that, in spite of one of the tidiest mobs we've had in ages, we didn't really get going today. Maybe there were too many chiefs, maybe we just expected them to roll over, but we didn't give them the hiding they needed. It could've got properly out of control today. We might've made the news – but as it is, we had a run of the mill scuffle with a few game woollies and that's about the size of it. Our one saving grace is the size of the train BR have laid on to get us all out of Wrexham. It's like a Man.U special.

I shy away from plans for a night in Skid Row and slink into the back compartment of the train, where the quilts are still babbling excitedly about John Kerr's goal. I sit quietly by the door and slip off the train at Neston, lurking in the shadows on the platform until it trundles away.

19 November 1979

It's weird being up this early on a Sunday. I've tried turning over and going back to sleep but the madly jubilant church bells and the braying of the Mostyn House brats put paid to that. I ended up staying in last night. I'd thought that Molly'd be in and we'd just nip out to The Old Quay and have a smirk at all the dolly birds, but she'd already gone out. I hope she's not falling for any of these spotty knobheads I see her chatting to at the bus stop.

Not only was Molly out, so, too was Dad. I doubt he was off anywhere interesting, nowhere he's in any danger of enjoying himself, but even if it's just the Indoor Bowls A.G.M., he's out on a Saturday night and that's something. I can't be sure whether my pleasure at this is down to a natural interest in his wellbeing or our increasing discomfort in each other's company. I didn't notice it at all when Mum was alive, but we have little to say to each other, me and Dad. On my good days I realise that he's had the heart ripped out of his life with next to no warning, and this subsequent flight inside himself is to be pitied. But most of the time I find him remote and disapproving. I don't suppose that he likes me very much and I've never really stopped to consider what I think of him. He's my dad.

Dad comes in halfway through *Match Of The Day*, grunts a few unkind and inaccurate remarks about Duncan McKenzie, then hobbles out. He's not fifty, and he has the beaten demeanour of an old man. I don't even realise he's gone to bed until the football has finished. I wait up until after midnight, changing channels, waiting for Moll to come home, but there's nothing on. We usually go for a drink of a Sunday afternoon anyway, so my questions can wait.

I'm up too early, pacing the house, wondering whether Dad's up, wondering if I should take him breakfast in bed. He'll probably think I'm after something, though I can't think when I last asked him for anything. Certainly not money. Gilmartin's doesn't open until eight, so I decide to take a walk along the front.

I get as far as Chompers where a sullen young lad catches my eye. He's standing outside church, hating being there, standing on the sides of his shoes in protest. His mum, a looker for her age, clips him gently and tells him he'll scuff them. I'm transported to my first day at St John's Primary, Rock Ferry. I'm four and three-quarter years old and I'm standing in the second row at Assembly, my first Assembly ever, during which the headmaster, Mr Bolton, is telling the big children to be extra careful with the new, little children, especially in the playground. What I'm feeling is not so much alienation as fear and, more than anything, hatred. I hate all the other kids in my row. I'm looking round at the various new boys and girls, despising them. Him because he has a huge, chocolate drop-sized mole on his cheek. Her because she has patches of rough skin. Him because his hair's too shiny. Two places to my right, though, is a lad I'm not going to kill. Him, I am going to befriend. He has style. He stands out because he's cocking his head to one side as he listens, contemptuous, letting the sides of his shoes take his weight. He looks like he can fight. Michael Reilly and I are to become as thick as thieves during my two-and-a-bit years at the Johnny's.

The surly boy is shepherded into church and I stand in abject misery on the old sandstone harbour wall. Mickey Reilly and Rock Ferry seems a million years ago. It probably didn't happen. Where's my life gone? Where's it going? Looking across the grassy marshland to Flint and up the coast to Point Of Air, I start to wonder what all those poor fuckers

19

in Wales are doing with *their* lives. Screwing? Sleeping in? Debating whether to take breakfast in bed to their broken fathers? Unlikely. They're probably doing what the gilded folk of Hollywood are doing, or Kowloon or Port Elizabeth. Worrying. Worrying about getting old, or about work, or about money, or about their boyfriend, mistress, lover, house, health, future. Life is shit. There is no fucking point to any of it. Not now that we've evolved past the survival stage. Maybe we used to live to hunt to kill to eat to live another day. Now we just kill time in as many sophisticated ways as possible. Pointless jobs. Pointless lives. Work. Television. Football. I look across to Wales and I think that the hills are nice. I'll go over there one day and just sit there, for a whole day, and see no one and not say a word. That'll be good. But right now I just feel bad.

I traipse back to Gilmartin's and buy the papers. *The Sunday Express* for Dad. *The Observer* for Molly. And *The Mirror* for me. *The Mirror* is about the only one of the Sundays to give Tranmere a regular write-up, otherwise I'd stick with *The Observer*, too. Mrs Gilmartin is delighted to see me, as she has been for the twelve years we've lived in Parkgate, though her clucking maternalism is these days tinged with too much fucking sympathy. Some days I really cannot stand the way she gives me those tragic, lingering looks. I feel like screaming 'I'M FINE!'. Which would really rest my case.

'And how's little Molly?' sings Mrs Gilmartin. Five-footten, I think, but don't say.

'She's fine.'

'Is she courting?'

Mind your own business you salacious hag.

'Studying too hard for that, Mrs G. I'm starting to worry about her!'

'Ho, she'll go far, that one. You both will!'

I smile my assent as Mrs Gilmartin, like she has done for

twelve years, pours two two-ounce measures of pear drops into two paper bags and presses them into my hand.

'Don't go telling all the kids!'

'I won't!' I laugh. Then I'm out of there.

I read all three lots of sports pages and to my ineffable joy there's a small piece in both *The Express* and *The Mirror* about the trouble before the Wrexham game.

> *Riot police had to be drafted into Wrexham, North Wales yesterday to quell vicious fighting between drunken soccer louts before yesterday's F.A. Cup tie between Wrexham and Tranmere Rovers. Police blamed the trouble on Tranmere supporters, though they admitted that they were taken by surprise by the numbers of fans travelling from Merseyside. Fighting spilled from the town centre to the area around Wrexham's Racecourse Ground, where mounted police with dog handlers managed to break up the rival groups. There were 2 arrests, mostly for public order offences.*

Both reports are almost identically hysterical and go on to list outbreaks of trouble at other F.A. Cup ties. I feel a glow of satisfaction. We're there in black and white on the news pages, next to Margaret Thatcher and Richard Branson. Chelsea and West Ham and Leeds will be reading this. The Pack are famous!

So buoyed am I by this that I rustle up sausage butties and individual pots of Darjeeling and take Dad and Molly their breakfast on trays. Molly is not amused at being woken at 8.35 a.m. and waves me away until guilt prevails. She sits up, calls me back in, gives a watery smile of thanks and asks me to leave the tray by her bed. I know it'll still be there, intact, when she wakes up at half-eleven.

I get a shock when I go into Dad's room. He's kicked all the sheets off his bed and he's lying there, absolutely naked and dead white, dead still. Not even snoring. I know he's dead but I feel nothing more extreme than curiosity. Was it an overdose? Natural causes? Can one actually die of a broken heart? I go closer. His legs are painfully thin – smooth and alabaster white – and his hairless buttocks have fallen and flattened out. Maybe they were the first bit of him to die. I wonder if any parts of me are dying right now, or have already died. I wonder if he has left lots of money. I might be rich.

I jump back as Dad sits bolt upright and for the first time in my life I hear him swear.

'Whaddafuck!' he blurts.

I always think of 'fuck' as being a *now* sort of word, but there it goes, out of his meagre mouth and off on its arc through infinity. He looks at me, crazy, as though I'm an intruder, a complete unknown to him.

'Brought you this,' I say, placing the tray at the foot of his bed. He pulls his sheets defensively around him, still eyeing me weirdly. I nod at the tray, inviting him to tuck in, and turn on my heel.

'Happy Sunday,' I say, on a whim. I bound downstairs to read the ag reports all over again before detaching the offending pages for my scrapbook.

20 November 1979

I'm sitting in The Copperfield with my boss, Bob McNally – well, boss in so far as you can *have* a boss at The Inland Revenue, PAYE Division, Birkenhead Office. Bob's a very agreeable sort, very unhappy with his lot in life and very insistent on his Mad Mondays down at The Copperfield. Most people celebrate birthdays, paydays, Fridays, whatever, but Bob reckons that a few large Jamiesons at the start of the week makes the remainder seem less painful. At 25p for Doubles on a Monday, it seems like sound advice.

Bob's keen on advice. He's especially keen that I should not end up like him, a Civil Servant for twenty-seven of his forty-three years. He describes this, quite rightly, as a modern tragedy and, since Mum died last year, has taken it upon himself with missionary zeal to steer me through the troubled waters of the last year of my teens. He'll offer advice about everything, Bob, and a simple request for paperclips can result in him quoting me tracts of Kant. He's forever on my case about living a *meaningful* life, twisting his face into a semi-aggressive, semi-pleading mask of wisdom. It's weird being philosophised at by someone who looks as crap as Bob does. He's five foot five, always wears slightly shiny navy blue slacks with a white shirt tucked in and the cuffs rolled with geometric precision to his forearms. What there is of his receding hair is cropped into a vicious, spiky Bruce Foxton swede, without the long bits at the back, while a singularly shit razor-blade ear-ring in the left lobe shows how little of a fuck he gives. Bob's teeth could well have been sharpened with a file. What often perplexes me about the badly-dressed is the

amount of thought and planning that goes into looking this
bad. The fussy cuff-length, for example. Does Bob think that
that looks good? I've never asked him.

'Dink about it, Paul, lad. How many *rarely* brilliant times
have yeah had in yeah life?'

Darlington away last season, I think. Both the Chester
games. The Doncaster scrot who gobbled off Baby and me
behind a pub before the pre-season friendly. It's easy, this. But
I nod my head sagely, smiling at Bob's earnest face and his
almost caricature Scouse accent. He's got a *rarely* mad voice,
old Bob.

'Dis is da lonely tragedy of da lumpen proleteriat. His truly
joyous moments in life are signposted by da sly shag, da
summerolidee and da Christmas piss-up. He spends all yeer
anticibatin one or dee udder. You can do better, Paul. Much
better!'

The last word sounds like he's coughed up a volleyball of
sputum. *Betteh*!! I go to the gents and contemplate my fizzog in
the mirror. He's got a point. I'm a sexy cunt. I certainly don't
need to wait around for Christmas snogs and drunken holiday
flings. The fullsome mop of orange hair is an immediate
eyecatcher. Not *ginger*, mind, not red or copper, this is a full-
on orange wedge, a bequest from my gorgeous, insane Irish
mother and only slightly helped on in all its teeming
magnificence by the occasional dollop of henna. And my face
– you'd say I was pretty if not for the nasty inch-long scar to
the left of my top lip. Again, a gift from Ma, this time with her
Claddah ring. Sex, and the getting of it, is not something I've
ever had to fret about.

But I *dink* I get Bob's drift. What he's railing on about is
seizing the moment, embracing the now, having an *actual* good
life rather than always working towards better days or
imagining them in retrospect. 'Pay no respect to retrospect.'
That's one of his, the funny little man. I stare directly into my

own big, liquid, pale green eyes and see no reason why I'll have to.

As I return to the bar, I see Bob trying to entertain three women with a story. They look tense, waiting for the rude bit then the bit where he asks them what they're doing after work, but they needn't worry. Bob doesn't hit on women. He's devoted to Janie and has almost certainly never kissed another woman in his life. He's a pretty subtle act, though.

'You, my derlin, are a liddle fucken belter. Yeah fucken *ger-juss*. Whatcha say yeah name was?'

It's that last bit that gives the game away. It must be obvious that he's taking the piss – out of himself, out of the situation, out of the whole rite of 'chatting up' birds in bars. He's standing over one of the women who's, what? Thirty-six, maybe. Even sitting down she almost comes up to his chest. She's smiling patiently, but there's still a suggestion that she thinks Bob's for real – not that he's working round the clock to put her at her ease.

'Look at her, Paul. Isn't she *gee-er-jee-uss*?'

The woman's wearing a delicate, white *broderie anglaise* blouse through which the outline of a black brassière is just visible. Mum always used to warn me that any girl who wears black under white is a strumpet. But this lady is no tart. Everything about her – the simple string of amethysts highlighting her naked brown neck; the gently unkempt tumble of her hair; the straight, alert posture – suggests a quiet sexuality, a confidence, a knowledge. Her skirt, in particular, tells out her understated self-possession. The skirt is black and almost ankle length and dowdy, but it is slit to the thigh, displaying long, slim, bare legs. She just sits there, quiet, as Bob jokes and slobbers. The woman winces at me confidentially. Her face gives very little away. She just smiles and lets it all happen, waiting for it not to be so. There's something else there, too, that universal flicker of, hmmm – *desire*? I think so.

I know so once we return to the table of Cartesian

deconstruction. Twice I look over at the women on the other table. First time she catches my eye for a second and gives me a lovely half-smile, then she's distracted by whatever her friend is telling her. Out of the corner of my eye I see her nodding politely at her friend's story while still glancing over at me. I pretend to be fascinated by Bob, oblivious to her attention. Next time she catches me, holds my gaze and stares right into me, so deep and real that it scares me. But I don't look away. There's no turning back.

Bob drinks up and fishes his shiny suit jacket off the back of his chair. I tell him that I might stay for one more. He follows my eyeline and throws back his head in mock disdain.

'Oooh-no! No you don't! No way, Paul, matey . . .'

'Come 'ead, Bob. Play the white man . . .'

He's a hard sell, that Bob.

'Dis is da lass time, Paul. Da lass time. Gorrit?'

'Nice one, Bob.'

'My arse! Dass yeah lot after today. Finito. En fucken joy it. Coz tamorra yeah cummen in, yeah given me all da derdy deedails den yeah pudden in a ree-quess for promotion. Yeah gunna gerra grippa yeah life! Geddit?'

I nod. Apologetically, formally almost, I go to join the woman. She's called Suzy. Or Susie. Somehow I like Suzy. Her friends, annoyingly conspiratorial with their meaningful glances, get up but don't leave, far too thrilled by this little dalliance, and determined to hang around for every last vicarious kick. I wish they'd just fuck off and leave us to it. Eventually they go.

Suzy and I chat idly. Somehow she gets the subject onto wine – she makes her own or she's just got some of the new Beaujolais or something. I'm hardly listening. My throat is thickening and the apex of my stomach, just where it deltas into my groin, hurts each time she leans over the ashtray and lets me look inside her blouse. She lives in Oxton. We get a taxi there.

I know the Oxton bedsitland well. Elvis has a place in Reedville and one of my first true romances from Birkenhead High lived in Columbia Road. It's a pretty bohemian enclave, Oxton, populated by Classics professors and potheads alike. I'm nonetheless taken by surprise by Suzy's tiny cottage, tucked away behind Poplar Road in a bumpy unadopted lane. I didn't believe places like this existed outside of the Cotswolds. She's got it dead comfortable inside, lots of tapestry hangings, floral wallpapers and loads of cushions all over the place. She's a bit of a hippy.

We haven't spoken a word during the short taxi ride. She stares fixedly out of one window while I slump down low in the seat, trying to look relaxed. I'm thinking how best to play this, trying to work out what she's likely to want from me and deduce that it's nothing more than the youth of my skin. She's expecting a rhino-horn erection and a vigorous walloping and probably thinks she's going to be teaching me the subtleties of love over a ten-week home tuition course. She's in for a surprise. For a boy of nineteen I've done a lot of sex and I know the value of shock tactics. As soon as we get inside the door I'm going to push her up against the wall and have her there, like that, with her skirt up around her waist. That'll be what she wants.

As though guessing my plan, she leaves the door for me to close and goes straight through to a small, quarry-tiled kitchen. I follow. She bends to select a bottle from the wine-rack, seeming to leave her bottom swaying slightly and for a moment too long, but suddenly I'm not so sure. My instinct is to just go up behind, get my hands all over her tits and get that skirt up over her head and just give it to her, maybe do her arse. But I don't know. All my confidence goes with that one, brief hesitation. She turns round and hands me a bottle of Beaujolais and a corkscrew.

'Want to do the honours?'

She can't keep the irritation out of her voice. She's taken a half day off work, brought some kid back to her place and, far from the afternoon of eager sex she anticipated she now has to talk to me and tolerate my opinions and feed me wine. I might be imagining this. Something has changed, though, and I can't get at what it is and I just want to be out of there.

The wine is smooth and heady. Suzy is very laid back, which only makes me more nervous. I feel as though she could just as easily sit and talk all afternoon. She knows a lot about music and puts on a soothing LP of Erik Satie piano nocturnes.

A tribute to awkwardness, I come back from the toilet and sit next to her on the little couch and start kissing her and caressing her throat. She's completely noiseless. Nothing pleases or displeases her. I'm aroused by this supine complicity and tug her blouse out from her skirt, perhaps a little anxiously, and work my fingers under her bra and, restricted by the underwiring and my position on top of her, try to get at her tits. She places her hand over mine and smiles kindly. Time's up. Her look says it all. I didn't quite get it right. I'm a sweet boy. Maybe next time . . .

Suzy can see my disappointment. She looks embarrassed, a bit ashamed of herself as she watches me lace up my shoes and shows me the door. I could probably still make up the time at work if I'm lucky finding a cab. What advice is Bob bloody derdy deedails McNally going to give me about *this* one, then? Suzy opens the door, still looking sympathetic and sorry, and brushes my ears with her lips.

'I like to be forced,' she murmurs. Shit.

I don't even get to the end of the lane. I hop through the gap in the crumbling sandstone wall of a big, spooky house and jack off furiously behind a holly bush in the bottom corner of the garden, coming quickly and wiping down strands of spunk with a dockleaf that I tear from the overgrown border. I don't feel so bad now, at all. Indeed, by Bob's definition, things have happened today. Experiences have been had. I've had a *rarely* brilliant time. Still tipsy from the fruity red wine, I head down to The Shrewsbury to wash my knob properly and see who's there.

With events turning out as weirdly as they have today, I've completely forgotten about the draw for the next round of the Cup. As soon as I set foot inside The Shrew there's Tony Byatt, Christy's horrible little brother, holding up *The Echo* and grinning twistedly.

'Halifax away! Sound, eh?'

Not really, I think. Not as good as, say, Huddersfield or Preston home, or a nice market town like Shrewsbury or Hereford to invade. But Halifax away, yeah, it's okay, far enough to seem like a day out, near enough to convince the floating voters. What's more, Halifax are struggling badly this season and with them now comes a very good chance of making the Third Round and the possibility of a real prize scalp. Tony and I while away an hour bickering over who the fantasy tie would be. He goes for all the obvious ones – Liverpool, Man.Utd, Aston Villa and so on, but I argue that those teams have got so many quilts that you'd never get to their boys. Manchester City'd do me fine, or someone like Middlesbrough or Leicester, teams who are going to bring the numbers but who'll have a little scout round, as well. We both agree that Everton'd be the worst draw imaginable, as so many Tranmere heads follow Everton, too. All the trouble with the Odgies, rightly or wrongly, is identified with a particular Liverpool firm from Huyton. They're the ones who came over for the Watford game. To me, though, you can't differentiate. All Scousers hate everyone. It's just the way they are.

Tony starts talking about their Christy's birthday do. It's tonight at The Brighton. It was mentioned at Wrexham, but I'd clean forgotten about it. I don't really know Christy Byatt, at all. I like him, he always seems like a good laugh and he's into the whole Irish consciousness thing, but I suspect he's had me down as a bit of a no-mark from the start due to me being from outside of the Woodchurch-North End-Downtown clan, or whatever.

No matter. I don't need big excuses to find my way down to The Chelsea on a Monday night. They've started calling it 'Alternative' night, which means that you might get to hear Gary Numan or Kraftwerk next to your Sister Sledge floor-fillers. But what it really is on Monday nights is Schoolies Disco. The place is completely rammed with little darlings, fourteen- and fifteen-year-olds in suspenders acting like porn stars on the dancefloor. The ouncers at The Chelsea call this mob The Young Ones and there's been many a story about the main doormen, Richie Givens and Barry McGrath, getting involved in some pretty unsavoury deeds with them.

I'm every bit as keen on the older girls in there. They don't flirt so much and they all look brilliant with their extreme, asymmetric wedge hairstyles, white Fred Perry shirts, little kilts and Kickers or Pod shoes. Clones, as we've wittily named them. Clones that give you no encouragement whatsoever all night then quietly ask you home for sex. The young girls in The Chelsea, though, they're pure jailbait. All they wear are these enormous white or pinstripe grandad shirts, stockings, suspenders and heels. Lots of them still have their hair long and loose, the better for tossing about to Roxy Music tunes. 'Dance Away' is The Young Ones' anthem. They all get up on the stage, legs wide apart, and take the piss out of the slack-jawed gawps round the edge of the dancefloor. Elvis and I do okay in here. We employ some pretty revolutionary techniques. Uniquely among the lads in The Chelsea, we will actually dance and think nothing of getting up for four or five tunes in a row. Getting in the thick of the action gives you an unsurpassed close-up of all the fanny – essential groundwork if you don't want to disappoint yourself later on. There's nothing worse than putting in all that spadework with a pretty girl then finding she's got a fat arse when the house lights go up. Up on the floor is the only place to weed out the probables from the possibles. On odd occasions some of the less sophisticated element from Leasowe have tried to make us look foolish, doing exaggerated, effeminate dances right next to us, but they soon get bored. There's very rarely any trouble in there. What there is is girls and guaranteed sex. So, yes – I'll be there for Christy's do.

A phonecall and a short walk takes me to Elvis' flat in Reedville. His place is cool, worth the hike up four dingy flights of a peeling Georgian townhouse. He's got the entire top floor and, apart from the little kitchen, which he hasn't really bothered with, the apartment is impossibly arty. You just wouldn't even think of doing some of the things Elvis has done with his rooms. He's made the most of the high ceilings with the usual big yucca plants, but his furniture and colour scheme is complete melodrama. The main living-room is dominated by a gigantic aquarium – twelve feet long at least, and almost head height. It's a riot of squiggly life – neon tetras, guppies and lugubrious loach by the dozen, patrolling in shimmering shoals and lending a dazzling sheen to a spectacular room. Elvis has plastered the wall opposite in a kind of golfball effect and covered it, floor to ceiling, with navy blue glitter – the stuff you sprinkle on Christmas decorations. He told me once that he robbed every single container from every stationer's in Birkenhead. It took him eight months. It looks fantastic. To the left and right of the non-utilised cast iron fireplace are his pride and joy – the Bang and Olufsen speakers which amplify his quirky tunes on an almost constant basis. I love coming round here. I could never have a place like this.

Elvis is listening to the *Apocalypse Now* soundtrack when I get there. He opens the door, grins, ushers me in with a flick of his fringe and carries on rattling out the bits of dialogue just before they're due to come. I liked this trait in him at first, his obsessive love of hip movies, and I tried to learn a load of the good lines from *Taxi Driver* and *The Godfather* and that, but now he just does my head in saying: 'Oxton. Shit. They were still in Oxton,' all the time.

I wash my armpits, clean my dick properly and rifle his wardrobe. I'll be staying here tonight, as has become customary, so I fold my work gear over a chair and look for damage limitation with Elvis' astonishingly unsubtle collection of sweatshirts. He's in a good mood, actually preparing a scran for me. Well, toast, optional Marmite on the side.

'Hooker comes up to a Scouser in Lime Street,' he shouts through from the kitchen. 'Fancy a blow-job, she says. Dunno, he says. Will it affect me dole?'

We settle into an argument about the relative merits of The Clash's new album, *London Calling*. Elvis thinks it's the best thing they've ever done.

' "Lost In The Supermarket", man. And "The Card Cheat". Fucken gorgeous songs, man. This is a band coming into its prime. This band'll just keep getting better and better.'

'Not exactly rock, though, is it? 'Sjust not The Clash to me. It's just self-indulgence. We like reggae so you're gonna like it. We've discovered Lovers' Rock with our new rasta mates so now we're gonna write a song called Lovers' Rock. And guess what? This'll slay yah! It is Lovers' Rock! '

'Ah, you're just trying to be contrary. You're scared of them becoming too popular and your kid sister liking them, eh?'

'No!'

'Sure you are. Always happens, doesn't it? You discover a group, go to all their gigs when there's no cunt there, buy their first records and wonder why you're the only cunt sussed enough to be into them, then . . . boom! They crack it. And you don't wanna know any more.'

This is tosh, of course. There's some brilliant stuff on *London Calling*. 'Guns Of Brixton' is pure Clash genius. But it all sounds dangerously mainstream.

'They'll be conquering America and doing jeans adverts next.'

'Bollocks!'

Elvis winks and tickles me under the chin. Most annoying. He sparks up a one-skinner and ushers me to my feet.

The Pack are all meeting in The Travellers, just down from New Brighton station, so we head straight there to get the Subbie Section of the evening over with. Buy Christy a drink, slap the boys on the back, convince each other we got a result at Wrexham, speculate about Halifax, then out. It's bad press on the chick front to be too closely associated with a big crew of boys in The Chelsea, though it does no harm to let them see you're connected. The bad boys still turn them on, but it isn't cool to act the laddo in a place like that.

Not that Christy and Co. seem too concerned. The moment we step into The Travellers, the atmos stinks. Batesy is by the jukey putting on 'Message In A Bottle' seven times. I fucking hate that band. The singer looks about forty and dances like a bad student divvy. I can't see how anyone can take them seriously. Batesy seems to identify them with the New Mod thing, but there's nothing new, modern or good about The Police. Batesy barely looks up, studying the jukey carefully before selecting The Police once again.

'Egwemont and Seacombe are meant to be coming down.'

This is pure Batesy. He lives for rumours about supposed rumbles, but you always want to hear his story, all the same.

'How come, Batesy?'

He nods over at Christy, Hardy, Kev The Man and Baby, all bolly-eyed, all savagely drunk.

'Them bell-ends. Been caning it down The Bwyton all afternoon, calling all sorts. Even Marty said he walked in and walked stwate back out again. He's chocker with them. Got us into all sorts of lumber.'

'Fuck that, Batesy,' scoffs Elvis. 'We've heard all this, before, haven't we? Fucken Seacombe this, Seacombe that. Fucken Egremont! Who are they? A few fucken rednoses. Fucken plazzy gangsters, the lot of them. Deal a bit of weed and they think they're the fucken boys. Who the fuck are they!'

Batesy turns round from the jukey, his eye still flickering from Saturday.

'We're not talking Bully and Fitzy and them little knob-heads. Oh aye – they'll be there once they know they're in with a chance, but our kwoo've upset the wong people this time.'

Elvis and me are laughing madly, now. Elvis puts his arm round Batesy.

'Batesy, just tell me. We are talking Wallasey here? Not, like, Rio or Naples or the fucken Bronx? Who the fuck is going to give us any grief in *this* yard?'

Batesy pauses for dramatic impact.

'Alfie Noble?'

Elvis and I gape at each other.

'You're joking . . .'

The Nobles are not a family to mess with. They supply all the ouncers and, therefore, the drugs to the clubs and pubs around Wallasey. Alfie Noble also owns several bars himself, of which one is The Brighton. He's officially in Construction, which could mean anything, but his reputation is for ruthless governership of the minor empire he controls.

'What happened there, then?'

Batesy is now warming to his role of Chap Who Has All The Lowdown.

'Well, they're in The Bwyton, wite, and everyone's having a smirk and they all love each other. Then Ali Noble comes in and takes over at the bar.'

Elvis is already burying his head in his hands. The Brighton is a medium-sleazy pub in Vicky Road which the Nobles have acquired and tarted up under some sort of Enterprise Regeneration Zone scheme. Alfie has given the place to his daughter, Alison, to run. Ali Noble is one of the all-time beauties of recent legend, an Untouchable whose misfortune it

34

has been to be squired by a whole succession of over-muscled porkheads, acquaintances of Noble *père*. Ali is a goddess, and Christy Byatt has become more obsessed by her the more she laughs off his requests for a date.

'No more. Please,' groans Elvis.

It's all horribly predictable. Christy has been chatting away merrily to Ali, making her laugh and challenging her to arm-wrestles, at which she is adept. Christy, who can veer from Mr Jolly to Mr Nasty in the space of one pint, returns from the bogs and starts expressing his desire for the lovely Alison by repeatedly calling her a slag and inviting her to get her dad down and anyone else he cares to bring. Ali is not too upset by this, but suggests that the boys have had enough to drink for one afternoon, at which point, far from restraining and protecting their pal, Hardy, Kev and Baby proceed to smash up the pub.

'Did she agree to go out with him?' laughs Elvis.

We go and find Marty to get a measure of how serious all of this is. He shakes his head in silent disdain.

'Very poor show from Tranmere, that. I don't exactly warm to the Nobles myself, but I can live side by side with them. I've dug these pricks out of some holes before, but this . . .'

Christy, Tony and most of the Tranmere contingent in the pub choose this moment to launch into one of Tranmere's sadder fighting songs. Marty hisses and swigs deeply on his pint. I don't understand him. He always sounds so measured, almost a principled man, then you'll see him bludgeon some cunt with a housebrick.

'One night in gay Pa-ree! I paid five francs to see!'

The singing has become raucous. Marty has to shout in my ear.

'You can do one, you know. No one seen you come in. I would if I were you. Not like it's your battle, is it?'

'A big fat mar-ga-ree!!'

This really gets my back up. Does he think I don't know

what he's saying? He's saying all sorts of things, none of them good. Sure, he's including Elvis in his Royal Pardon, telling us that he's on our side if we don't fancy underwriting Christy's little spat with The Mob. But this is all about Belonging, and Marty, in as nice a way as he knows how, is asking me why get my nose busted when I'm not even invited to the party? This is for the hardcore, the boys who've known each other forever and no matter how far I'm prepared to go for The Pack it can never truly get me in. Fuck him. I've been going away with Tranmere for over two years now and I've never shit. Even when Stockport surrounded their shitty little station at the end of my first season and came at us with basies, I was right in there next to Marty. I seem to remember one Christy Byatt hiding in the storeroom. But he's one of the good old boys and that's that. Elvis, who's originally from the Ford, looks like he's going to smack Marty. He manages to keep his voice even.

'Come 'ead. He's right. This is nothing to do with football.'

'So fucken what! Fuck that! We stick together! We walk down there together and we see what happens!'

Elvis shakes his head and looks at the floor.

'Let's see what fucken happens, Elvis.'

He sighs and looks pityingly at me.

'What you drinking?' I ask him. I believe I see Marty grin to himself. Elvis comes and joins me at the bar.

'Carty – only go if you *want* to go down there. If you feel that sort of loyalty to these cunts. But don't act how you think Marty wants you to act. D'you know what I'm saying?'

I know what he's saying. And he's right. But I *want* to go down there.

As is often the way with these things, nothing happens. Marty chats amiably with Richie Givens on the door and, after a tense initial period of studied nail-biting and sussing out the supposed Seacombe names, everyone settles to their own thing. The main part of The Pack retire to the back room to sing long songs about sexual prowess and violence, while me,

Elvis and a wobbly Baby Millan go to the dancefloor. I see John Godden arrive with Alfie Noble. They're straight through to the champagne bar. It's not so hard to guess what's afoot. John, who rarely goes out, has been summoned by *Il Cappo* to put his house in order. It crosses my mind that John, from Downtown, might even relish the job after the way Christy led the charge on Saturday in front of all the old Woody heads. We'll see.

A Young One is giving me the eye. She's *very* young, this one, if she's fifteen it's only just. We dance to 'Electricity' by Orchestral Manouevres, a Monday-Night favourite down here. She says she likes my sweatshirt. It's a violent turquoise with a big fuck-off INEGA in purple right across the front. Very Elvis. She complains about the heat and the crowding which I take as a bid for a half of lager and lime, but she says no, let's go outside for a bit. In the demi-light of The Chelsea's lobby I see her properly for the first time.

Cute, but, frankly, not long a woman. She's got a beautiful little arse, knows it and works it insolently as she walks ahead. Her long brown hair's tied back in a ponytail and her white Lois sweatshirt is tucked in to show off small but shapely breasts. Barry McGrath gives her and me a leer as we pass on out of the club, offering one last reminder that she is *young*. I don't care. She's cool and knowing and I've still got Suzy on my mind.

We're on the promenade, walking slowly, huddled reflexively against the winds slamming in off the Mersey.

'Still too warm for you?' I gasp through shivering lips. I left my jacket in the club's cloakroom so I wouldn't have to pay twice. It's bitter. She snuggles tightly against me.

'Look at that,' I say, pointing to the yellow-lit waterfront and the wild, murderous tide. 'Makes you feel . . . *tiny*, doesn't it?'

I mean it, but I'm trying to show her a sensitive, romantic side to my nature. She slips a hand into mine and as I'm resigning myself to a snogging marathon with maybe a bit of tit over jumper, she tugs me by the hand.

'Shall we go up here?'

I can feel the surprise my face must register. She leads me over to a gap in the railings into Vale Park. No messing round. She sits down on the slope, I join her and she starts necking me. We've been kissing for all of five seconds when the hand that isn't stroking my cheekbone and scratching my scalp is reaching for my zip and working my knob outside the gusset of my briefs. Good job I washed the blighter.

'You're not very hard.'

I find this a distinctly unerotic utterance but I soldier on, pulling her sweatshirt out of the waistband of her jeans. No bra, and there's barely any give as I set about her smooth breasts, kissing and biting them. I'm getting there, but I'm still not fully erect when she pushes me down and starts flickering deftly at the shaft of my cock with her tongue and scraping my balls with her fingernails. I allow myself just to lie back for a second and think up the weight of Suzy's big tits in my hands and that shocking final pay-off.

'*I like to be forced.*'

How the fuck did I fail to pick up on that! I am now bone hard and the Young One is getting to her feet. In the queer moonlight she looks pale and beautiful as she raises her slender arms to slip off her sweatshirt. She stands on one foot as she pulls off her jeans and for a moment she is in front of me, perfectly white and naked except for the brief panties which only accentuate her flat, narrow stomach and smooth hips. She steps out of the knickers. Thank Christ! A compact shadow of mott – I thought she was going to be bald! She fixates on my swaying knob and stands astride me, bends and grips my dick and strokes herself with the tip. A sharp gasp and she lowers herself until I'm right inside her and her knees kick tight into my sides. I try to reach up for her tits but she jerks her head back and holds my wrists, bucking urgently and cursing me in soft soprano.

'Yeah bassded! Yeah fucken little bassded! I'll screw duh fucken dick off yeah, yeah little . . . fucken . . . get!!'

It's too much. My knob's going to explode, she's so fast and tight. I can't stand it. I throw her over onto the wet grass and start to ram her. I can't stop myself. She moans quietly, girlish sighs followed by long howls of shame, then she murmurs to me.

'Don't come inside me, baby.'

This serves only to trigger a ferocious ejaculation. I pull out, coming thickly over her stomach and ribs. I lie back and watch my cock flop, finished, to one side, still pulsing spasmodically. I reach for her, but she's already up and dressing. I watch her step into her knickers, possibly in love, when she speaks again.

'Arr-ay! State of me kecks! Spunk fucken everywhere! I can't go back in there now – you'll have to walk us home!'

I explain that I can't do this because I have to go to work tomorrow and my office clothes are at Elvis' and I have to stay at his. She seems pacified by the fact that I have a job, an office job at that, but she can't see why she can't come back to Elvis' with me. I promise, meaning it, to meet her at The Chelsea on Wednesday. Her name's Lilly.

I find Elvis sitting in the champagne bar with Marty and John and Richie Givens. Marty, a completely different man to the pensive model of a few hours ago, greets me like a brother, introduces me to Richie as one of the good 'uns and fills me in. There's been murder at the club. John has bottled Christy after he refused to go back and apologise to Alison Noble. Elvis sits tensely as Marty glories in his story. Tony Byatt and the rest of the Woodchurch crew have gone mental, slamming any known Liverpool heads in there, including some who are alright, then turning on the outnumbered ouncers. By the time Richie has called down more fellas from The Oystercatcher in Leasowe, The Pack have gone wilding down the prom, attacking cars and mugging punters coming out of The Grand and The Guinea. Marty and Alfie drove after them, trying to calm things down, but the SPG have been on the scene. Must've been some shag. I didn't hear a thing.

Elvis is silent as we walk up Vicky Road for a cab. I'm not sure if he's chocker with me for keeping him hanging on at The Chelsea. I couldn't've been away more than half an hour, but I ask him, anyway. He says it's just The Pack, they depress him. He tells me that Godden whacked Christy as he was turning away from him. He had no chance. Elvis reckons The Pack are going to be split over the incident. I tell him The Pack's been split for years. Whatever, I can't see myself coming back to New Brighton in too much of a hurry. I toy with the notion that I should've let Lilly come back to Elvis', but that wouldn't have done at all.

24 November 1979

Port Vale are a difficult mob to make out. Up until recently they had a bit of respect in Third Division circles. There's been seasons when they've brought six or seven hundred on a foggy Monday night, quite a few snarlers, too – but then there's been games where only one coachload of quilts turns up. Tonight I strongly suspect the latter will be the case. Although it's a Friday night and The Potteries is only ninety minutes away, we played them in the League Cup back in August and gave them a severe hiding, home and away. The return leg up here, in particular, saw The Pack being extremely badly behaved. It's hard to see Vale coming back in a hurry.

In the away leg on a sweltering Saturday, about seventy of us hop off the train at Kidsgrove and dawdle up there. It's some walk to the ground and even in our summer attire of Fred Perrys, canvas F.U.s and yachting pumps we're mad hot and ready for a drink by the time we get to the ground. We go to two or three pubs in the vicinity and just get stared at, then at about half-two it goes off. Loads of us are sitting on the wall outside this pub enjoying the sunshine and, personally, I'm starting to hope for a lazy ag-free day. Then there's a commotion inside the bar, accompanied by a stool crashing out through the main plate-glass window. We jump up and run inside, to see Batesy and Eddie Spark penned in at the top of a little raised balcony with about twenty Vale trying to get up the staircase. Batesy and Eddie have hauled the fruit-machine to the top of the stairs and, as we come in, they're rocking it to and fro, trying to topple it down onto the Vale crew. We fly into them. The lad I'm about to smack gets it full in the ear with a pint pot, courtesy Mr O'Connor. Elvis stops, mid-mêlée, as though the action has been freeze-framed, and points right at the lad's face.

'One man lost an ear during the trouble,' he says in a batty Pathé News voice, then starts fighting again at twice the speed of anyone else, butting some poor fatty over and over again until he goes down. All the time, Elvis is pulling these crazy faces and adopting mad fighting stances. I swear he thinks he's in a movie most of the time. Busies are called to the scene. The stricken pub manager points frantically at Eddie Spark as we leave for the ground.

''Im!! 'Im!! 'E were one!!'

We block the door as Eddie scarpers then make our leisurely way into the overgrown away end. The Juniors surround us excitedly, handing out Adidas T-shirts and, bizarrely, Puma wrist-bands. They'd stayed on the train until Stoke and ragged the shops in Hanley. After the game we're surrounded by a legion of surly plod who are none too happy about having to march three miles in uniform in this weather just to protect the good folk of Burslem from us thieving scum. Anyone so much as stepping into the road is given a bit of truncheon, accompanied by the timeless police mantra:

'Behave like animals you can expect to be treated like animals.'

Vale bring hundreds to the return leg. In classic subby, woollyback style they pile off the coaches in three foot-wide Birmos, blind drunk, singing their heads off and holding their arms out dead wide. I'll never know why these subby crews sing so much. Pricks.

The problem for Vale that night is that there's only two turnies on the coach park side of the Open End (Vale *always* come by coach), slowing down the flow of their mob into the ground. As they trickle in, they're immediately being hopped on by us. The wools outside the ground can see what's happening to their boys and start trying to surge the gates.

They wait this side of the turnies until they get about a hundred together, then they all run onto the Open End, howling like Comanches, expecting us to scatter. We don't. Vale are still coming into the ground. The police are running all over the place trying to break up all the little battles that are going on. It must look smart from The Cowshed. The Busies are really wading in hard.

Most of The Pack start to mob up behind the kiosk. Mistake. The plod have now got them in one place and succeed in baton-charging them back down the slope and across the corner into The Paddock. It's relatively easy to contain them in there. They just throw a double line of uniforms right across the corner of the Open End and, truncheons drawn, whack anyone who comes too near. Seeing that they're safe, Port Vale now bounce right up to the police line, gobbing over and giving it the woolly fingers to The Pack. They reckon without twenty or so of us still dotted around the Open End, some good heads, too. We silently let on to each other, me, Elvis, Baby, Godden, The Spics, Batesy, Eddie and a good few Juniors. We go single file right behind the Open End and round the side to the kiosk. Vale are ten, fifteen feet below us with their backs to us, jumping up and down in front of the Busies, making like they're going to burst through on Tranmere.

Marty spots us from The Paddock and starts screaming for us to get into them. John holds us back, telling us to wait. The Vale knobs start to turn round. John's face is twisted, spit flying everywhere.

'DZUH! RO! VUZ!'

Although there's loads of them, Vale freeze. The ones nearest us start pushing each other forward. That's it. No one has to be told. We fly down the terracing and tear right into the thick of them, lashing out with a flurry of boots and fists. I see Baby's blade come out and next thing it's the parting of the Red Sea. Vale do not want to know. They won't fight. We're

43

booting them everywhere. Some of them are jumping over the hoardings and legging it onto the pitch in sheer panic. From then on it's mayhem. The Old Bill turn away from The Paddock, allowing The Pack to swarm back across into the Open End. More and more Vale fans are vaulting onto the pitch, with others trying to hide in the bogs and behind the out-buildings. Numbed against pain in their terror, some of them take a running jump at the perimeter walls, clinging onto the barbed wire for leverage. It's a bit sly. Some of them are fellas in their thirties with no interest in knuckle, but the Juniors still pull them back down into the ground and slam them. It's weird seeing grown men crying like that. In the aftermath, shellshocked Vale fans are still wandering around the side of the pitch, waiting to be told what to do by the plod. One young Busy tells me it's the best ag he's seen in three years policing Liverpool, Everton and Tranmere.

Today there's the usual rumours from Spuds and The Free Library. Vale are out for revenge. They're bringing three coachloads of loons to The Rockvilla and coming looking for us. How the fuck do these rumours start? It always ends up with some lad's sister who's married to a lad from whichever town you happen to be playing who overheard the leader of their firm saying exactly what travel arrangements have been made. I know people just want to spice up boring fixtures, but it can backfire. Only this year, Easter Monday, we had Carlisle at home. Some mate of Baby's *assured* us he had a mate at the AA who'd phoned him to say four coachloads were on their way. We decided to really shit them up by going up to the M62 and ambushing them, but Elvis and Marty managed to convince us that we'd just look like beauts. We still spent an hour and half waiting in The Ship so's we could hit them as soon as they came down Borough Road. Carlisle brought precisely thirty-two fans that day, in unmarked cars.

I phone Maggie at The Library to see who's in and she puts me onto Batesy. Batesy tells me they're all going to wander down to The Rockvilla just in case and I try to persuade him it's a waste of shoe leather. As an aside he tells me that the Woodchurch are boycotting Tranmere after Monday night's nonsense. He doesn't believe it, himself. I'm not so sure. They can be very insular, the Woody. It'd be tragic after the way The Pack's started to take off this season. Without the Woody, Tranmere are nothing.

I get off work at 5.00 and trundle down to The Carlton, where I always meet Elvis before home games. I'm early, so I nip over to Maguire's for the *Echo*. Although Tranmere's game is tonight and Liverpool and Everton have stunningly uninteresting games tomorrow against Coventry and Ipswich, there's no mention of us on the back page. Tranmere, as usual, are an afterthought on the inside back page. I don't know why I bother with the *Echo*.

A couple of little darlings from Birkenhead Tech come in. I know them vaguely from Rupert's, where they've got a bit of a rep as Nosh Queens. Seems it's a privilege extended to the ouncers and a handful of Names – and if you're Tranmere, forget it. One of them who I think is called Sonia smiles across. *All* Tranmere, I wonder. Some prick who's still wearing Pod sidles over to them, but doesn't stay long. Must be a lecturer, dressed like that. Sonia half beckons me over with a slight flick of her head. I'm well aware that girls like this love making cunts of lads and come equipped with a bag of tricks to make you look pathetic. A favourite is to ask you what you do for a living then, the moment you speak, stifle a mock yawn and just get up and walk off. But they're chicks, these two. I think what the hell and pull up a stool.

Sonia is indeed called Sonia and her mate's name is Jackie. Jackie is very nervy and chatty and, of the two, slightly more, well – *tarty*. They're both gorgeous-looking girls but where Sonia is pale and turquoise-eyed and beautiful, Jackie is brash and suntanned and wears a ton of mascara around her huge, brown, oval eyes. And while Sonia seems content to listen, Jackie talks breathlessly about one subject. Lads.

'You knock around with Mark Elways, don't you?'

'Elvis? Yeah. He's me bezzie. How d'you know Elvis?'

'Always out, isn't he? Seen 'im today. State of that new swede of his.'

This is news to me. Jackie traces an imaginary astronaut's helmet around her head with her two hands, cupped.

'He's got this big mad bowl 'ead, with a, like, full moptop fringe at the front and a mad sticky-out bit at the back and it's dyed, like, *pirple*.'

Bastard! We saw two lads at The Swinging Apple with these hairstyles last week. It was me that found out the cut is called a Mushroom Wedge and we agreed that we'd both take the plunge together tomorrow. We're booked in at Minsky's for three o'clock, with the operation not expected to last more than an hour, thus allowing time to get home, get changed and get back out without the new barnet sagging too noticeably. It's never the same after you've washed it, no matter how many home-styling accoutrements you have. Typical of fucking Elvis to nip in first.

I convince the girls that the *pirple* to which Jackie refers is probably plum and that the plum Mushie is going to be *the* haircut to have. I let Sonia know that I had the first Wedge in Birkenhead and that Elvis used to dress like Lou Reed when I first met him. She smiles beautifully, barely raising her top lip. I fall in love with the gentle dusting of freckles on her nose and the single tiny beauty dot above her lip and the way she sometimes looks down when you're talking to her. By the time Elvis strolls into The Carlton trying to look demure with a planet-sized purple-pink upside-down fishbowl hair sculpture, I'm smitten by Sonia. Depressingly, her eyes seem to dance a little more brightly when Elvis spots us and comes over. She makes room a little too readily for it to be strictly ladylike, and he plonks himself down. His hair shudders. Sonia leans into him as she talks. Bastard. I must make a note to wear more mauve in future. Jackie and I chat gamely and try to have a laugh.

'We'll all have to go out in a foursome, eh?' she says, hoarsely, sparking up another fag. 'No strings, mind! No fucken hankypanky!' She screeches with laughter at this not notably amusing remark. We hug the girls warmly and jog towards the white floodlights of Prenton, still an uplifting sight after all these years. To our surprise and considerable joy we've missed nearly ten minutes of the first half. The surface is too scarred and greasy for either team to make an impression. Elvis and I drift into speculation about whether the Woody will indeed turn their backs on Tranmere and we reminisce over legendary sightings of imaginary mobs. Half time comes quickly for such an incident-free contest.

The attendance is poor. Not only have Port Vale brought no support whatsoever, but neither, it seems, have Tranmere. We stand in the usual spec at the Bebington end of the Borough Road stand, but there's none of the heads to be seen. No Marty. No Batesy. Certainly no Christy or John Godden. Me and Elvis are The Pack. Thank fuck Vale haven't brought anyone.

We're getting by on crowds of about 1,800 at the moment and a decent mob of aways can swell that closer to 2,500. 3,000 is a bumper gate. Tonight there's scarcely more than 1,200 here on a night that is, allowedly, wretched. The wind is vicious and the rain is starting to slat in at that unique Tranmere speed and angle that makes it feel like a storm of javelins. Nonetheless, Tranmere are a few straight wins away from the promotion places, so tonight's turnout is miserable. Maybe people just don't want or need a third team on Merseyside. Maybe the *Echo*'s judged it fair. Elvis and I stand shivering in our Adidas kagouls, arguing about the virtues of Nastase training shoes over their ghastly, I think, yellow pretenders Forest Hills.

About nine o'clock the gates open at The Cow Shed end to let out the pensioners and the early-darts. In march The Pack in all their rain-sodden glory, forty, fifty of them, dressed up and soaked to the bone and, in spite of Monday and everything, a sight to put a smile on your face. Most of the Woody crew are there, though no Christy. Marty tells us that they've walked round every pub in Rock Ferry in search of Vale. They're definitely here somewhere. John Godden's cousin saw them all in The Little Chef by the A41. There's a pause while this sinks in, then we crack up laughing.

Things are decidedly weird after the game. Elvis and I have got into the habit of walking up to The Halfway House for a pint after the game, while I'm waiting for the F23. He can easily cut through to Oxton from there. As we're walking up Woodchurch Lane, there's the bang of big shop windows going in behind us. A chant goes up:

'All the Woodchurch!
Stick together!
All the Woodchurch!
Stick together!'

Fifty yards back down the road there's a crew of Woodchurch, some of whom were not inside the ground. Christy's there, with Tony, Hardy and Baby. They're grappling with the big steel bin outside the chippy. They get the bin out of its foundations, take a few steps back and launch it through the chippy window. The place is still busy with sensible Tranmere family-types queueing for spring rolls and what have you, but no matter to the Woody. Crash! Sounds of consternation and disbelief from the customers and the ricochet of dozens of running feet as they stampede up Woodchurch Lane, laughing hysterically. Christy's little firm must be on sulphate, they're wild as fuck. Hardy passes within a few feet of me, spaced out, a scary figure dressed in the long tweed overcoat that's becoming very cool with the over twenty-five ex-punk element. He doesn't even recognise me as he jogs by, pointing ahead at the bus stop. There's a little group of Thingwall lads who go away with Tranmere but tend to steer clear of The Pack. Elvis looks concerned.

'What d'you reckon?'

'Dunno. Taking the piss, aren't they?'

'Hard one to call. You know what they're like.'

'It's Sammy Dean and that, isn't it? Colin Bullen? They're not going to start on them, are they?'

'Dunno. You know what they're like.'

I know what they're like. Years ago when I first started coming to Tranmere, I used to cower in the corner of the Halfway House bus shelter, praying that the Woodchurch contingent would carry on walking past and not bother to wait for a bus to come. More often than not they'd pass by, maybe snatch some quilt's scarf or slap some cunt on the back of the head. Every now and then, though, you'd hear them arguing in the distance about whether to jib the bus, and as they got nearer you could hear the voices getting louder and then they'd stop, right behind you. They were getting the bus. It's only three stops to Woodchurch but if the bus was late it could seem like an eternity. You'd dread one of the twats catching your eye.

'Where yeah from, lad? Lenz ten pence.'

I remember one sad spotter from Greasby staring intently at the floor, desparate not to offend. One of the Mini WEBB, a little skin aged about ten, lay down on the pavement directly under Greasby's eyeline so he couldn't avoid looking at him. He jumped up, feigning outrage.

'Fuck are *yew* looking at, yeah little puff. Giz yeah fucken jacket!'

The lad took off his jacket meekly, snivelling gently, eye-contact still avoided. Nobody went to his rescue. They were bastards, the WEBB, and still are, but that's the sort of cold-eyed mettle that makes every crew in the Third rabbit-scared of Tranmere.

'Come 'ead,' I shout to Elvis and run after them. Elvis shakes his head and lollops halfheartedly behind me. They've surrounded the five Thingwall lads, who, to their credit, are facing them down. Hardy's frazzled mind is a bit confused by this, and I know that if I get in quick he'll be content to let them off after diplomatic intervention.

'Wo! Hardy! Baby! 'Sgoin on, lar?'

Baby gives me a horrible fucking look which I file. Hardy isn't exactly welcoming either, but he's too whacked to know the difference. Elvis catches up and gives the Thingwall Five a greeting that is hugely matey, considering he barely knows them. Nice one, Elvis. The tension is dissolving. I turn to Col Bullen.

'Been The Rovers, Col?'

Colin nods. Of course he has. Why the fuck else would he be standing at this bus stop at half-nine on a Friday night? I offer this *a posteriori* evidence to Judge Hardy.

'You know Col and the lads, don't you, Hard? Good lads these.'

Hardy clearly doubts their pedigree, but seems prepared to give them the benefit of the doubt. A current of disappointment passes through his rank and file, deprived of sport again. They begin to trudge off, one or two of them giving me a little pat on the shoulder and a 'See yeah, lar'. Baby Millan brushes past with Christy and Tony, Hardy jogging to catch them. They go into conference as they walk down Swan Hill. I'm pretty sure the subject is me.

As my bus pulls away, I glance back at Elvis, waiting to cross at the lights. To my considerable merriment, his new swede has been completely flattened by the rain. He looks like Norman Bates, stalking the rainy sidestreets. I can't wait for tomorrow night.

26 November 1979

Today is a day I've been dreading. Today is one year and one day since Mum died and we're off to a memorial service at Landican to pay our respects. Molly's genuinely frightened about having to return to the cemetery. For a good month after the funeral she had vivid nightmares involving her own prolonged incineration. We've both talked about getting out of going somehow, but we know it'd slay Dad if we weren't there. He's been using the old 'I don't ask much of you' sketch and keeps referring to Mum as 'your mother'. Molly and I have been using it all the time, these past few days. Last night as I was getting ready to go out, Moll came into my room, took a tour around my spongy new Mushie Wedge and shook her head, tutting:

'Your mother wouldn't like it!'

The plan last night was to find Sonia and Jackie, take them back to Elvis' and paste them so vigorously that I fall into the sleep of the forgotten and somehow contrive to waken too late for this memorial. A more outrageous flight of fantasy would be hard to conjure. Finding them is a breeze. As we walk into Rupert's the pair of them are hanging round the two grocks on the door. Jackie gives us the faintest smile in response to our effusive greetings while the feline Sonia turns her back and starts whispering in the other ouncer's ear. He rocks back on his heels and laughs gruffly, casting me a disdainful glance. My ears redden and I start to feel extremely foolish standing there in Lois bib 'n' brace, blue Kios boots and an outrageously homosexual hairdo, while the bouncers chuckle at our discomfort and the girls completely blank us. *All* Tranmere? I think so.

Elvis doesn't seem so distressed by the knockback.

'Pair a scrots anyway, lar. Dunno why you're so fixated with 'em.'

'Me! You were going on about Sonia all through the second half last night! And the other one! It wasn't *my* idea to have a foursome . . .'

Elvis smirks crookedly.

'I'm very modest in that respect,' I state.

He laughs at this.

'Conservative almost!'

He's shaking his head in disbelief at me.

'So you wouldna done it?'

'Weee-ell . . .'

He guffaws and claps me on the back and tries to persuade me to come see Prag Vec and Gruppo Sportivo at Eric's. I'm tempted. My Mushie looks ten times as good as his and some of the older, vampish birds in Eric's are horny as fuck – but the hiatus with the nosh-to-rule queens has focused me back on the memorial. I'll get off now, do the right thing, please Dad, be a good son. Elvis is understanding and doesn't even try to pressure me. We walk as far as Hamilton Square together, where we end up facing each other on opposite platforms. We pull mad faces at each other. Elvis pretends to throw up, much to the consternation of all the couples at the far end of his platform. My train comes first. I salute Elvis as it pulls away from the platform. He looks quite happy to be going out on his own. Maybe the Nosh Queen plan *was* my idea. Maybe Elvis is going where he really wanted, after all. I get off at Birkenhead North and am grateful to find the Wrexham train already in.

So I'm lying here, a gammy mug of hour-old tea congealing by my bedside, wide awake and wholly dreading the day that lies ahead. I can't get up. I've tried the usual litany. 'If you get out of bed on the count of five you'll get Liverpool in the F.A. Cup.' Works for me during the week. I can get up for work, no problems. Never been late yet. What isn't helping me today, is yet more crazy thoughts. I think mad things all the time. Sometimes I'm sitting with Dad and I start to feel lightheaded and I'm sure that any second he's going to reach over and strangle me. I have a real struggle to act normal and make my excuses mid-conversation and rush outside for air. A lot of the time also I can't help but reflect that every action I make takes me a step closer to death. My compulsive listening to 'New Dawn Fades' by Joy Division can be taken as a mitigating circumstance but it doesn't deflect from the truth that by the time I reach the bathroom I'll be that little bit further down the road into the Valley of Death.

I'm just wondering what proportion of dead people, in universal terms, reside at Landican Cemetery, when Moll taps at the door to see if I'm up. Molly, who is already the most beautiful girl in the world and will have accounted for dozens of lovelorn saps by the time she's sixteen, is also the wisest person I know. She reads situations perfectly, gets right to the marrow of every question. This morning she sees that I'm just feeling blue and sluggish and, more than anything, scared. She heads me off like a kid.

'Come on, Paul. Let's get this over with and we can start looking forward to Christmas.'

Christmas! Just around the corner yet I've barely given it a thought. Office parties! Sex in stationery cupboards with married prudes! Crewe Alexandra away! God bless you, Molly, I'm up!

In spite of having violently scrubbed my teeth before and after breakfast, I'm conscious of my stale breath from all the beer last night. It doesn't seem at all right to enter a House of God with pungent halitosis, so, just as we're about to leave I run back upstairs to the bathroom. I smear toothpaste all over my gums and pop my toothbrush into a pocket. I'll give them another going over just before we get out of the car. As I bound down the stairs, another brainwave hits me. Pernod! A double-edged sword, this – I can calm my mounting nervousness with a soothing pastis and cleave the scum off my palate in one fell swoop. Then, fumbling with the screwcap, a yet better idea. I empty the dregs of a little bottle of Hunts tonic, open an almost full bottle of Schweppes peppermint cordial and pour two inches into the empty container. The car's horn beeps angrily. Come on! I add a further two inches of Pernod. Almost there. I fish out a robust blue bottle of Domestos bleach. Got to be careful with this. This is the stuff that'll zap those smelly lager bugs lurking in my guts, making me fart and stink. But too much and I'm in trouble. Just a hint, however, a *soupcon* of household bleach and I'm re-born as Fabio Freshbreath. Beep! Beep! I hear Molly's elegant footsteps picking their way up the pink gravel. This is for you, Mum! Salut! I top up the elixir with tap water, shake the bottle hard, knock back a slug, roll it round my larynx and expel it into the sink. Whoo! Mr Minty! Let's go lament!

'What the hell are you *doing* in here!' hisses Moll, rather crossly.

'Just slooshing, Moll. Slooshing for Jesus. C'mon. Let's go.'

The much-dreaded memorial turns out to be a moving, satisfying experience. It forces me to remember things I'd buried and suggests an aspect of this last year or so that I wasn't aware of or simply hadn't bothered to think about. This whole business of Tranmere and The Pack. I see now the time I knew for sure that Mum was dying is the time I started hiding in their midst, looking for a new outlet, a way of expressing myself. Not that I really felt like saying much. I wanted rude action. I wanted out of school. I wanted a job and money. I wanted stuff that that was me, mine – nothing to do with this plan Mum and Dad had mapped out and which had now proved terribly fallible.

It's not a big revenge deal or anything premeditated or evil.

You just think that you can get away with things. Or don't quite care as much. Or maybe you have a different take on what's fair, what's right or wrong. Something changes, anyway. There's no big scream, no desperate cry from the heart, just, something goes out. Something's turned off.

That happened the evening I went straight from school to the cancer ward at Clatterbridge and held her emaciated yellow hand and knew for sure that there was no way back for her. I didn't wait for Dad to come in the car. I wanted to walk back, all the way, by myself back through the lanes. I felt solitary and special. No kid at school was going through this, or would ever have to. I would never now have a single thing in common with those complacent, protected, inexperienced *boys*. I walked for miles through the dark lanes and I felt great.

Today, there's no church, or sermons or hymn-singing. We attend Mum's immaculate grave – how often must Dad have been down here – and lay fresh flowers and stand in silence for a moment. Dad holds Molly's hand. I think he'd like to hold mine, but he knows I won't feel comfortable with that. He smiles at the pair of us, seeming to say that, you know, it's not so bad here after all, is it? You needn't stay away. Come often. He starts talking to the grave. Not out of embarrassment but because it seems like the right thing to do, Moll and I withdraw a few paces. I can still just about hear him mumbling away.

'Our Molly's coming on a treat. Top in French and Drama by far. Second in English. 92 per cent. I ask you. Still insists she's going to drama school. Still going to be an actress. Don't think she'll change her mind, now.'

Molly winks, but I'm incredibly touched by this. He's so strong in all his frailty. So simple, serene and happy. Will I ever be happy?

'Our Paul's doing very well at work. He's putting in the overtime and he's been told to apply for promotion. Hasn't been there a year and a half. How about that, Patsy?'

I know Dad's not proud of me and he's only mentioning me now to seem even-handed, but I can't help feeling moved by his words. Not so much that he's being nice about me, but that he's standing in the open air talking directly to my mum about me, their firstborn. I gulp and bite my lip. I've never seen myself as sentimental. Far from it. I find it difficult to express basic emotion in a one-on-one situation. I can't show pleasure at birthday or Christmas presents, even if I'm delighted with the gift. Once or twice one of my colleagues at work has suffered a bereavement and people will rally round in some way, show their sympathy and support. Not me. I'm not overtly hostile, of course, but my stance is, like, sad but everyone's gonna die. And then I start asking my sorrowful workmates if they knew the victim personally. Most of them think I'm either sick or trying to be controversial for the hell of it. I'm not. It's how I really feel. But I feel okay about this, now, crying quietly while Dad talks to his dearly beloved Patsy. I don't recall whether I cried at the funeral. I remember noticing a lot of people who I had never seen before blubbering passionately. But this feels normal.

At Dad's suggestion we go home via New Ferry and stop outside the first shop we had. In the late Fifties, before Spar and all those convenience stores, Mum had the idea of a General Stores that sold *everything* and was open eighteen hours a day. She met Dad at The Grafton and, an unlikely combination of mildness and madness, they just flipped for each other. Hardly spent another night apart until she went into Clatterbridge for the first of her radiation sessions. Dad, crazy about music and poetry, wanted to open a beat-café in one of the arty neighbourhoods – Bold Street or Lark Lane. Patsy, brought up off Duke Street among rogues, wanted out of Liverpool. As a kid she went on a day-trip with all the other urchins to the salt-water pool at Parkgate. Parkgate was her destiny. That's where she was going to live, even if it meant working twenty-five hour days. And that's where she came home to die.

We sit in the car outside the old shop, while Moll encourages us to reminisce. She doesn't remember the Rock Ferry years at all. All she has known is Parkgate and nice people and ponies and fresh air. I'm a little troubled by my memories – I mainly recall violent arguments between Mum and Dad. Dad tells how he begged the bank manager for a five-hundred-pound loan for stock and how Mum had insisted that we spend every penny on a dazzling selection of goods. Not just crisps and packs of Walls bacon and Wonderloaf bread in its wax paper with squiggly edges, but every imaginable shade of Dylon in its little tin packs and Terry's Spartan chocolates and potato-peelers with orange binding round the handles – things we would never expect to sell but which Mum, with her knowledge of real, working-class necessity, knew would fly out of the shop.

Now I see it better, me helping unpack cartons of cigarettes – Sovereign and Number 10 and tiny packets of Park Drive Filterless Fives. The sight of so many boxes and cartons of goods used to send me mental with excitement. I was the same at school. A big new box of chalk or a ream of paper would make me giddy. I remind Dad how he'd let me cut open the cardboard cartons of crisps and Five Boys chocolate with a slice-sharp craft knife and I'd gasp at the sight of all those goodies within touching distance. For all that we had King Solomon's mines on the premises, I wasn't allowed to eat sweets or crisps. They relented a little with Molly, but she wasn't that bothered about sweeties.

A couple of years later the store had done so well that they could up and move and carry on the successful formula in Neston. They could've opened a chain of shops if they wanted, gone on into supermarkets, but Dad always said they were content with what they had. In my early teens I used to slate him for his lack of ambition, for being a loser, and I'd watch his gentle, intelligent face twitch with hurt as Mum would come hollering at me and bang me round the room with a tablespoon, just as she'd been meting out the discipline forever.

I'm sorry about all of that now, but it's too late. I've seen the films and read the books and I know that fathers and sons are meant to have some special lifelong bond. I suppose I broke ours a long time ago. I've probably messed up one of the few good bits about life. Molly gives my hand a little squeeze as we drive off, happy that I'm indulging Dad in his memories.

We spend the afternoon in The Malt Shovel and have a good laugh. Dad seldom drinks, but Mum was extremely popular in here and we've come to celebrate her life. Dad is genuinely funny when he tells his stories and I feel even worse about shutting him out this much. Maybe it's never too late to make amends.

Molly drinks too much rum and blackcurrant and starts flirting with the in-breds in the back bar. Just as a ruddy-faced fisherman is getting too close for my liking, Moll clamps her hand across her mouth, too late to prevent a geyser of purple spew from spraying all over the randy prawncatcher. He stands there, lost for words, pointlessly wiping sick off his jumper with his own bare hand. Suppressing my mirth, I help Molly away, apologising to the flabbergasted fisherman.

'Your mother wouldn't like him,' I say to Moll as we exit The Malt Shovel. We stroll back down the hill to The Ropewalk where Dad stops outside our Sixties-built dreamhouse and announces that he's decided to sell it. Molly and I gawp at each other.

30 November 1979

Elvis calls just as I'm about to walk down to The Priory to eat my sandwiches. Even when it's freezing I've got to get out of the office at lunchtime and I'll usually take a stroll down to the river, or the silent grounds of Birkenhead's ancient ruined Priory, or just to the Square to eat my butties in solitude. I've never really got into the office pub scene, apart from my little tête à têtes with Mad McNally, though I was pleasantly surprised when I first realised how many really nice-looking girls there are here who regularly get drunk at lunchtime. Everyone must *hate* their jobs.

Today the sun is shining as bright and as high as a midsummer's heat haze, although the fresh breeze is keeping the air temperature cool. Still, it's shirtsleeves weather and I'm just beginning to contemplate a nice doze in the sunshine when there's Elvis, prattling away about how his cousin, Alfie, has passed his test and bought this old Triumph Herald and fancies a run out to Chester.

'Come 'ead,' coaxes Elvis. 'Fuck the desk job for an afternoon, man. Get on the tide. Go with the flow.'

I'm not so sure about this bogus surf-speak he's been dropping since we saw *Apocalypse Now* for the third time, but for once the prospect of jibbing work is most appealing. Doubly so as Bob has taken a rare day's sick-leave. This is a man who probably wouldn't give up a day's work for his Gran's funeral, so I'm guessing that either Janie's finally got pregnant or it's the return of the wretched gall-stones that plague him periodically. Bob and I have somehow got ourselves into a gratuitous work-ethic philosophy, trying to make sense of the minimum eight hours we spend in this building every day by brainwashing ourselves that we must show strength and discipline and put in the hours of graft – not for the government, the ultimate beneficiary of our labour, but for ourselves. We call people who miss work Softbellies, so something's afoot with Bob.

Elvis is saying they'll meet me in The Copperfield, but I don't want anyone to see me – not because I'm fearful of Bob finding out but because I don't want to hand back the moral highground.

'Pick us up outside The Central. Can you be there in ten minutes?'

He says no problem, but of course they're late. Standing there, transferring my weight from one foot to the other, I muse how much a part of my life Elvis has become these past couple of years. He's my best friend, for sure, a constant companion and opinion-former on everything from Wayne County's sex-change to the possible maximum number of buttons on the waistband of a Huddersfield fan's kecks. Yet I don't know him. And what I do know of him is not especially likeable. He's funny, witty in a cruel way. There's no one better at taking the piss, a trait I've found myself trying to emulate – with some success. He's got quite a hold over me, Elvis.

Although I'd seen him at Tranmere, doing his thing, for years, I really got talking to him when punk came to Eric's. Skeleton Records brought a few punk bands to Digby's in Birkenhead, most notably The Jam and The Vibrators and Motorhead, when they were taken up by the punks by virtue of their fast, dirty sound and repulsive frontman, Lemmy. But it was Eric's that had the cream. The Clash, The Damned, Generation X, The Stranglers . . . all of them came to Eric's and the under-eighteens were catered for with notoriously wild matinée shows.

I would see Elvis, eyes exaggeratedly wide and glamorous

with mascara, hitching by the tunnel or trying to bunk on the all-night tunnel bus, which was 40p even then. Once he nodded to me at the bus stop and I burned up with embarrassment. A few weeks later we both, along with twenty other kids, hid in the girls' bogs after an X-Ray Spex matinée and stayed there until the night-time show. It was unbelievable. Girls in bondage gear were openly necking each other on the dancefloor while a goonish lad with a toilet seat round his neck was given a wank up against the jukey by an anorexic witch-chick in a plastic mini-skirt. I was in love with the place, though I could never take to the clothes. Elvis sat in the furthest corner and smoked constantly, as though his dad owned the place and the crowd was a minor irritant. He resisted my attempts to catch his eye and vanished into the night after the Spex had finished a show of spellbinding aggression.

Out of Eric's grew a new Liverpool music scene. On Thursday nights any old shite with a long, pretentious name was given a platform. It was ten bob entry and they were quite happy to allow fourteen- and fifteen-year-olds in with the rest of the sparse attendance of misfits who showed up for Modern Eon, Pink Military Stand Alone, Those Naughty Lumps, Orchestral Manouevres In The Dark, Echo And The Bunnymen and The Teardrop Explodes.

I was transfixed by the breasts of Jane Casey from Pink Military as she sang the sexy-prepubescent chorus of 'Nothing Special', when Elvis appeared at my side.

'Too much, eh?'

It was. But I got over my nerves, told him where I'd got my Pod sandals from (Neil's Corner) and settled down at a formica table to talk about Joy Division, Elvis' contention that Curtis was ripping off Ezra Pound (I offered Sylvia Plath just to show that I knew a bit about bad, depressive poets) and the prospect of that gobshite Pete Wylie ever making it. I was actively downhearted when Kenny, the cuddly ouncer, took our

61

drinks off us and told us the club had closed a quarter of an hour ago.

But that wasn't it.

'Shall we go the Cazza?' said Elvis, already making off past Yates' Conway Lounge and away from the direction of the tunnel.

I'd heard people in Eric's talk about the Cazza, always in the context of post-club imbibing, and pictured a smoky cellar with arty people sitting on upturned tea-chests discussing semantics. I was desparate to go. I had a pound note and about thirty-odd pence in change, enough for two drinks but nowhere near enough to get me home. Besides, Mum was sick and I didn't want to give her more cause for worry.

'I've got poke,' said Elvis. I took it that this meant he had some influence with the doormen. He pulled out a thin fan of newish fivers, about sixty or seventy quid. I gaped.

'Here y'are,' he said, handing me a bluey. 'You can owe it us.'

We walked up Bold Street and Hardman Street and turned left at The Philharmonic pub into Hope Street, crossing to a terrace of elegant Georgian townhouses. Elvis led the way down the steps to the cellar of one, slightly jaded building where a dirty brass plaque announced: Casablanca Club. The Cazza.

It was smoky, drinks came by the can, music from a scratchy jukebox and serious pseuds sat on rickety chairs discussing Situationist art. It was magical. I loved it. The crush I had on Elvis when I woke up next day was as powerful as any feeling I'd had for any girl up to that point. I'd walked home along the railtrack from Birkenhead Park, where the tunnel bus dropped us and where we'd said our ta-ras, to the embankment near our house, a hundred and fifty-minute walk which seemed to take five, during which I luxuriated over our hungry conversations, my mind wired with thoughts and opportunities.

Elvis and I became very tight, very quickly. I think I gained more from those early sorties than he. He was, I quickly realised, the only working-class person I had regular contact with apart from my mum. He reminded me where I came from – or where I wanted to believe I came from. The glamour of a Liverpool-Irish background is vastly more seductive than the safety of the shopkeeper's son I now was, so I found my mother's accent coming out more and more, along with her confidence, her mordant wit and her violence. Elvis and I went everywhere together. Except Tranmere.

It bothered me back then, not that long ago, that he was embarrassed about integrating me with The Pack. I lapped up the stories, the awaydays, the characters, but the closest I came was to watch from the other side of the Borough Road Paddock as Elvis and Marty and Eddie and Co. piled in, week after week, building their rep via Walsall and Rotherham and Brighton and York. I could see that, as that whole Liverpool thing was beginning to build – the haircuts, the clothes, the snobbish, superior mentality that comes through being in on something good from the start – Tranmere was becoming a scene in itself. Every other Friday, new faces would turn up, all in the homogenous drainpipe Lois, every face semi-hidden by preposterous, dangling fringes. I wanted in.

It was Crewe away, a Wednesday-night game. I was meeting Elvis by Moorfields to go to Probe, who had a clear-vinyl 12" of 'Public Image' by PiL, Johnny Lydon's new group. I think the idea was that I'd take Elvis' record home for him, to save it getting damaged at Crewe. There'd been no suggestion that I was going to the game. We walked down Stanley Street, chatting about the girl from Stevie And The Stopouts, a Birkenhead new-wave group. Elvis reckons the girl who plays bass keeps giving him the eye. Reckons he just has to say the word. I'd be interested, normally, but I'm waiting for him to shut up so's I can tell him I'm coming to Crewe.

We cross Victoria Street by The Lisbon. Elvis tells me it's a benders' bar, as he has done about a dozen times. We amble up the three steps leading into the rotunda of Probe Records, all fake nonchalance, ready for the trial by haughtiness that buying a record from Probe entails.

Immediately the smell of patchouli hits you, a tawdry throwback to Probe's none-too-distant days as a head shop. It's easy to get sucked into the pseudo-obscure, underground vibe of these shops, but the knobheads they employ soon bring you back to reality. For years I used to pluck up the courage to go into Skeleton in Birkenhead after school. The head dope in there, a Bruce Foxton lookalike in a striped matelot shirt and a donkey jacket would clock your school blazer, wait for you to pluck up the courage to come up to the counter then, at that very moment, turn his back on you and start searching for a non-existent waxing for an eternity-seeming ten minutes. When he re-emerged and you asked him for a second-hand Velvet Underground or Can he'd look a bit disappointed that he couldn't sneer at your choice. Then one day I came in, he had his back to the shop, chatting happily to a scruffy mate up by the till, and I heard him say:

'Best fuckin record I've heard for fuckin ages, man. "Driver's Seat" by Sniff 'n The fuckin Tears.'

I cracked up. I laughed out loud and Bruce Foxton went red. Sniff 'n The fuckin Tears, man! Probe's still an ordeal, though.

A gaggle of leather-clad death-heads, each with fantastic black-varnished fingernails, black pomades and a multitude of skull rings and crucifixes, gathers in a conspirational hush by the counter. They stir momentarily when we walk in, briefly curling their lips in that familiar sneer reserved for any 'straight' who enters their sanctum, before turning back to the main gargoyle, a white-faced mincing mannequin who makes every minor purchase at Probe a penance. This amusing cult are known to outsiders as The Probies.

Elvis goes straight up to him. The main Probie, their leader, ignores him and drawls on about a handbag fight in The Masquerade.

'So we're in the Mazzy, right, and Kev – you know Kev, yeah, the hairdresser, right, from X-Tremes . . .'

He makes the word 'Mazzy' last half a minute as he wraps its sibilants round his teeth in the faux-effeminate style that has become hip with the Sefton Park crowd.

'Any danger of getting served, mate?' interjects Elvis, jauntily. The head Probie doesn't so much as pause to give him a withering look. Elvis simply isn't there, hasn't spoken, doesn't exist. It's the first time I've ever seen Elvis burn up. He doesn't look at me. For a second I think he's going to leave it.

'Ay, bollocks, I'm talking to you!'

This time the Probie hears. He sighs and raises an eyebrow at his coterie, and carries on with his tale.

'AY!!' shouts the Elv.

Before Elvis can continue, the white-masked freak has grabbed him by the collar and pulled him halfway over the counter. I'd heard that The Probies can have a proper go, but this is hilarious. A tranny dishing out the ag.

'Now lissssennn may-tee,' lisps the Probie. 'I'm having a con-va-sssayshun with meee matesssssssss. Shew sssum man-nerssss!'

He drops Elvis on the floor. Elvis gets up, mortally embarrassed, and dusts himself off to sniggers from the rest of the shop, ordinary, student punters trying to ingratiate themselves by joining in the merriment. This riles me. There's only one thing to be done, to regain the dented honour of my pal and, while we're at it, prove to him that I'm as handy as the next chap in a ruck. This is for you, Elvis. I run into the thick of the Probies and start lashing out, indiscriminately at first, the positive energy of my anger giving me a fearsome strength to slug it out with any cunt in there. The students and a couple of the Probies leg it out of the shop, shitting themselves. At this point it's like the moment when you dive in off the highest board. You know you're going to do it. You know what the effect's going to be.

I jump up onto the counter and hoof Lord Probie in the mush. His alabaster makeover cracks into fragments. I'm captivated, then strands of red blood prickle his face, following the course of the jagged map. I'm aware of Elvis laughing madly as I crack the sales assistant again then jump down, ready to scarper.

'Get the till!' laughs Elvis, breathless, hysterical. I see him head-butt one of the Probe crew full in the face. His nose blows wide open and he goes down, screaming. This sobers me. The poor lad looks shellshocked, standing there, in his own shop, bleeding.

'Come 'ead!' I gasp, grabbing Elvis and pulling him with me. 'Let's do one!'

Convinced that we're wanted by Interpol, Elvis decides he'll give Crewe a miss. He's sure that we're in big trouble as a result of this and we don't go near Probe or Eric's for ages. But we couldn't be more wrong. The next time we bump into Chief Probie he's fawningly pleasant and subsequently, though he regains his aloofness, we never have trouble getting the staff's attention in Probe. Elvis reckons that the middle class fear physical violence more than any single thing and any political party who can *guarantee* their safety will be voted in for life.

That night I laid low at Elvis' flat for the first time, smoking pure grass rollies and listening to *Coney Island Baby*, *Funhouse* and *Station To Station*. 'Wild Is The Wind'. What a song. What a pad.

My reverie is ended by the asthmatic parping of a bottle-green Triumph Herald – not the snazzy soft-top Vitesse model, sadly, but a well-preserved late Sixties jobbie which is not much less eye-catching. To my abject horror, John Godden is sitting next to Alfie in the front seat, frowning darkly as he always does. He gets out begrudgingly to lift the seat up for me. I scowl at Elvis as I clamber in beside him. John Godden is not a person anyone would choose to spend an idle day with in picturesque Chester and I'm quite sure that had Elvis mentioned this little matter to me I would be back at Birchen House collecting tithes for HM.

'A'right, John,' I say, jauntily, hating myself for it.

'A'right, Prof,' grumbles Godden. Twat. The only person who still calls me that. The Professor and, later, The Mad Professor were nicknames given to me by Marty when Elvis first started bringing me to aways with The Pack. In those days, I made no attempt to disguise my speaking voice, which isn't quite as coarse as the guttural Scouse of, say, Marty or Godden. The way I figured it back then, everyone should just be who they are. John Godden had a fucking muzzy, for fuck's sake and no one gave him stick for that! How could anyone ever think a muzzy looked cool? And how could anyone with a muzzy make a value judgement upon me? Still, by his insistence on still calling me Prof, Godden was making plain that, whatever feats I achieve with The Pack and however highly Elvis or anybody else thinks of me, to him I'm still a puff. An outsider. I'm alright, but that's as far as it goes. Which is just fine by me. You spooky, moustachioed cunt.

We set off along the A41. We pass our old shop in New Ferry. Conversation is stilted. I've met Alfie three or four times and found him instantly likeable and easy to talk to. Godden is the stumbling block. I take it that Elvis, like me is loath to talk about the usual subjects for fear of being branded a phoney.

'Ezra Pound! Fuck's he? Barnsley's chairman?'

Equally, none of us knows him well enough to ask about Christy or whether he's heard about the Woody ragging the Lane after the Port Vale game or whether he knows any good jokes.

'Here y'are. Pull over a sec!' he orders. Alfie pulls up outside a grocer's in Little Sutton. Godden jumps out. The storekeeper in me groans silently.

'Fuck's he doing now?' sighs Elvis.

'Fuck d'you bring *him* for?' I snap.

'Just happened, didn't it, Alf?'

Alfie nods, glumly.

'Just there at the lights by the library and he came walking out of The Ship and seen me sat here in the car and he's, like, ooh! A mo-mo car! Where you going, lads? I can hardly fuck him off, can I?'

I feel better that this isn't a pre-arranged case of The Goddens. He returns to the car, carrying a big tray of eggs. He sits back down in the front passenger seat and cranes his head round till he can see me.

''Ave a laugh, eh?'

I nod. I feel a bit sad that this great, respected warrior, one of the undisputed leaders of one of the hardest mobs in football, is trying to fit in with us, behaving in a forcefully, jolly way. I'm also a touch bemused by the eggs. What does he mean by 'have a laugh'? He doesn't keep us in the dark for long. As we get to Upton, on the outskirts of Chester, we slow for a roundabout. A scholarly-looking teenager takes an eternity to pass by on his cycle. Whomp! An egg lands smack between his shoulder blades, making a comical mess of his school blazer and causing the bike to wobble precariously. The schoolboy's ears blush furious red but he's too apprehensive to turn around and confront his agitators. We cackle horribly. Godden's right. It's a hoot, this egging lark. He leans out of the window as we go past the miserable cyclist.

'TRA! MEE! YAH!' screams Godden, making three syllables out of the word. The lad nearly falls off his bike again.

We go on an uproarious egging spree around Chester, childishly splitting into two teams and earning points for strikes against American tourists, who are thin on the ground, and suspected Chester fans, who are many. We nearly split our sides when John takes up a position on the old footbridge across the River Dee and scores a full hit on an oarsman rowing his sweetheart. He gets him full on the hooter, causing him to screech in pain and almost topple into the river. His girl seems to enjoy the moment.

We meet up on the far bank of the river, on the school side.

'Anyone got any eggs left?' I ask. Impatient, always, I've long since launched my quota at the unsuspecting folk of Deva.

'Two,' says Alfie, my team-mate.

'One,' says Godden.

Elvis holds his arms out wide and shrugs. I point to the bandstand across the river. There, hosting a jolly procession of Morris Dancers and a full brass band, is genial, evergreen television presenter Stuart Hall. He pitches a breathless stream of gobbledygook at the cameras and turns to the zanily attired dancers, who proceed to clout each other rhythmically with sticks.

'Weird!' shouts Godden, jumping up. 'Fucken too much, that!'

He watches, shaking his head, mouth slightly ajar. He hands me his remaining egg.

'Grab that,' he says, running back towards the footbridge.

We all look at each other and shrug.

'Pagan ritualists got the better of him,' smiles Elvis. 'Nut Crackers Stun Pack Nutter!'

We all chuckle. Godden comes into view on the bridge. He's running so violently that the bridge, a mini-Clifton suspension lookalike, can be seen juddering from here. He looks just the same as he does when he's leading a charge on a crew of aways.

Our attention switches back to the white-suited, white-smiling Stuart Hall. He's now in the thick of the Morris Dancers, gambolling with the best of them, grinning like a happy fool and singing lustily. It's some sort of Christmas wassail. I turn to Elvis and Alfie.

'Fifty points for Stuart?'

Alfie guffaws and gives cousin Elvis one of his eggs. 'One . . . two . . . three!!'

Our paltry volley of eggfire cuts through the air and takes an agony of a time to land. We take cover under the trees, peeping out like furtive Thunder And Lightningers to catch the results of our mischief. None of the eggs catches Stuart's suit or his smile, but one explodes vividly on his blinding white shoe. Another overshoots altogether, but our last egg makes a spectacular bull's-eye right on the Jester's shoulder. We collapse in a heap, shaking hands with each other and hardly daring to look up. When we do, a terrifying sight awaits.

John Godden is dancing frantically in the midst of the Morris Dancers, grinning and slobbering and flopping his head around. Some of the brass band and other onlookers are casting him worried glances reckoning him simple, or drunk, or both. Stuart Hall, ever the pro, makes his way towards him, still dancing, still smiling. He waves away a copper who's set to pounce. No need for any fuss. We look at each other and hide our faces in our hands.

Godden has got away from Stuart, whose path is blocked by two lines of dancers clashing batons. John reappears at the end of the row. He looks directly into one dancer's face and says something. The dancer agrees, smiles and nods. Godden decks him and takes his baton out of his hand. He takes his place in the phalanx and tries to get up to speed, imitating their athletic jumps and skips. He leaps up and hoofs his dancing partner in the face and cracks him across the forehead with his baton. Stooping deftly to collect his second baton, Godden curtsies to the next two dancers, bows down low then clubs both capering revellers to the floor, dancing around their senseless bodies and waving gaily at Stuart Hall.

'Come 'ead!' says Alfie. 'Let's get the engine running.'

Not a moment too soon. The music slows to a discordant mewl as the horrified dancers stand back to isolate Godden. The portly constable looks most reluctant to tackle him. Stuart Hall steps forward. We run for the car, which is parked by The Handbridge pub, not too far away. Alfie does a crazy reverse U-turn so that Godden will be on the right side for his door, as we wrongly suppose. Alfie tells us later it's because his rear registration plate is filthy and the numbers illegible. Godden emerges from the towpath, laughing and sweating, pursued by several bovine college-boys and the intrepid copper. Stuart Hall is nowhere to be seen. We cry genuine tears of laughter for fully five minutes. Godden childishly insists that we find a pub with a telly so's he can watch *Granada Reports*, and I feel a lot more kindly towards him after today's utterly barmy display. We all know that we'll remember this afternoon forever.

2 December 1979

Elvis returns to the canteen table bringing coffee and a bacon buttie for me and a mug of hot chocolate for himself. I don't believe I've ever seen Elvis eat anything – maybe a Pot Noodle, once. His flat is testament to his seeming desire to live out the whole wasted youth fantasy. There's cannabis plants, wraps of speed, sachets of mint-chocolate drink, hundreds of albums lining the glitterwall, of which a dozen or so Bowie bootlegs, imports and rarities take pride of place. Everything is elegantly wasted. This is not the habitat of a healthy man.

I stayed there last night as per plan. Not planned is the major sesh we have with Sonia and Jackie. Elvis phones me at work about half-five. I'm putting in some overtime to make up for yesterday – I do most Fridays, anyway. The office is pretty deserted after one o'clock. Everyone bails out to The Copperfield and The Post Office and not many make it back, so it's a nice, tranquil way of getting your hours up at your own pace. Elvis is calling from The Carlton and is highly excited.

'Carty! Listen, lar, get down here pronto! You want to see it! All the little darlings from Tech're in here with mistletoe and all that, pissed out of their swedes. The Nosh Queens are all over me, man, pallatic, asking where you are an' that and grabbing me stoggs and everything . . .'

Some encouraging signs admittedly, but, after the Rupert's débâcle, I decide to play it cool and finish my overtime first. Besides, if they're drunk now they'll be putty by seven o'clock.

I see them straight away when I walk in there. The Carlton is packed out with tinsel-clad students, necking, fighting and throwing up, but over in the corner sits The Thin White

Duke, smiling to himself as Sonia strokes him under the table and Jackie flickers her tongue in his ear. He looks pretty cool, Elvis. His head is almost too big for his shoulders and everything about his death-white face is gaunt and tragic-poetic – huge blue eyes, red, very red lips and that flat, Celtic nose. The cheeky cunt is wearing my black box leather that I left at his for tonight, but he looks fucking brilliant in it with a green beret pulled down over his brow. He takes a sip of his drink and touches the rim of the beret in greeting.

'Kin'ell, Carty, lar – took your time, didn't you? These girls don't hang around for *anyone*, you know.'

I smile at the girls and kiss their hands and apologise, putting on a stupid Roger Moore accent.

'Unspeakably rude of me. Please forgive me.'

Jackie and Sonia giggle coyly and flash me little come-ons. Elvis gets up.

''Cha drinking?'

I order a vodka and PLJ, knowing that The Carlton's about the only place that carries it, and sit down. Within seconds, Sonia is purring drunken profanities into my ear, seemingly suggesting that she intends to suck my prick while Jackie fingers my arsehole with her sovereign. Since the age of fourteen I've been familiar with all sorts of women, but I still don't quite get it that girls are just as obsessive about sex. I can't prevent myself from feeling that I've pulled off some sort of stunt when I get my hole and stuff like this still amazes me, the way that so many girls will do . . . *anything*. They're talking and acting like a couple of high-class whores, but it's just Sonia and Jackie from Birkenhead. I well remember when, in the fourth Year, Michelle Biley and I went for a walk in Eastham Woods near her house and she stopped and leaned against a tree and said that she'd do anything. That shocked me to the pits of my stomach and she had to offer me a sort of menu before I fully realised how far I could go with her. I probably would never have got so skilled at anal if not for dirty, rapacious Michelle. She *loved* to be bummed. Sonia untucks my shirt and runs the flat of her hand across the top of my groin. Elvis returns, smirking.

'Like what you hear?'

'Dunno,' I smile. 'They're ever so forward, aren't they. Strumpets!'

The girls crack up laughing much more than this puerile quip deserves, then Jackie apologises about the bouncer sketch at Rupert's. Her eyes are glassy.

'We're sort of seeing them,' she explains. I nod. The girls don't want any more to drink. Knowing what lies ahead, neither do I.

We phone for a mini-cab. Waiting outside, even in the half-light cast from the pub I can fully appreciate why these girls are so sought-after. They're both tall, for a start – it's unusual to find two such fine, long-legged specimens in an everyday yard like this. Sonia is perfect. Regardless of her reputed gobbling and other sundry sexual capabilities, you could just sit there and gaze at her sulky little face for hours on end. Tonight, though, Jackie, making full use of her height in kilt and suede ankle boots looks aggressively sexual. Her tits are stupendous, straining against a slightly shrunken black mohair jumper. I don't care whether I end up with her or Sonia.

Things go beautifully *chez* Elvis. He mellows the girls out with his Durutti Column album and a succession of pure grass one-skinners then, without any contrived 'pairing-off', he starts necking with Sonia. I swallow hard and look at Jackie. She gets up and offers her hand and leads me into the main bedroom. She gropes for the light switch which throws blue shadowlight around the room. Nice one, Elvis. I reach for her, but she pushes me back onto the bed.

'Wait. Watch.'

She puts a finger over her lips and gives a half-smile that makes me ache. She closes her eyes, drops her head back and begins swaying, legs slightly apart, caressing her breasts through

74

the spiky wool of her jumper, gently at first then more roughly, lifting them and rotating them and squeezing them together. She tugs off the jumper and flaunts herself at me, hands on her hips, tits unfettered by a bra but their darkness accentuated by a plain white singlet. She licks the tips of her fingers and circulates her nipples until they show through the fabric. Inch by inch she drags the tight cotton vest up her smooth stomach and up over her shoulders until her breasts are fully naked. They're miraculous, round and brown and heavy, yet scarcely moving under her touch. She moistens her fingertips again and strokes her nipples until they stand out. I can't sit here like this. I'm so hard, I've got to get her down and fuck her, I can't sit here a moment longer. I go towards her, unzipping my cock and pulling it out for her. She lets her eyes drop for a second and looks it over, then pushes me away.

'No. Wait.'

She puts her hand under her kilt and gives me the half-smile again. Her other hand pulls up the skirt, showing the same ultra-white boys' briefs. She moves very slowly over her mound, slipping a sovereign-clad finger underneath the knicker elastic. She murmurs something, eyes closed, and rocks to and fro in her suede booties. She lets out a series of short gasps and comes up close to me, placing my hand over my penis and whispering urgently.

'Now you! Now you!'

I try to go slowly and put on a show for her, but I can't take my eyes off her legs and her kilt and her breasts. I shuffle towards her, kecks still round my ankles, and put my hands on her arse, pulling her into me, grinding my dick flat against her stomach and searching for her tongue. It isn't offered. She pulls her head away and pushes me back.

'I can't screw you,' says Jackie, looking at the floor. 'I can't.'

I sit down on the bed trying to think of something funny to say, still manipulating my penis absentmindedly.

'Saving yourself till you get married?' I offer. Her face thunders over.

'Something wrong with that?'

My face must be a delight.

'No . . .'

'Well, then. Go and goose Sonia if you've got to get your end away that bad.'

I look down, uncomfortable. If I'd been looking at Jackie I might have seen a sly look pass across her adorable face.

'I didn't think you were like that . . .'

'What?'

'You know. Wham-bam, thank you ma'm. Shag-happy.'

I laugh and shake my head.

'That's precisely what I'm like.'

'See what I mean?'

'No. What?'

She imitates my voice.

'*Precisely* what I am. You're dead refined, aren't you? Got nice ways about you. Sort of . . . sensitive.'

The penny drops. I try to be cool and factual.

'Let's get this right. *You* – are a virgin.' She nods. 'And I am a nice, sensitive guy. *You* are quite prepared to stroke yourself off in front of me, but I am not allowed to touch.'

'Yet,' she smiles.

'And what about the ouncers at Roopie-Doops. Are *they* sensitive?'

She hangs her head.

'I touch myself and they toss themselves off,' asserts Jackie. I snort my disbelief.

'We get in for nothing, you know!'

She looks flustered and hurt. I go to her and hold her close. She falls into the embrace. My penis, insensitive to the moment, twitches and rises up her thigh. I let go of her and sit down on the bed.

76

'Do you want to go out sometime? For a drink or something?'

Her face is all sly victory. She beams and pulls back the covers on Elvis' bed. We hold each other for ages, but the heat of my cock fails to melt her. She lets me kiss her breasts and lick her spine and there's a stifled groan as I try to work my dick between her buttocks, but she's not having any of it. This from a girl who was going to finger my arsehole with a knuckleduster. She turns away on her side and pulls my arm over her and sighs happily.

Conscious that I might start snoring, I don't allow myself to drift off to sleep until I'm sure that Jackie's dozing. She begins to wheeze rhythmically, then lets out a fart. I gently move my arm from around her. She farts again. She's sound asleep, but now I can't settle myself. Still aroused and frustrated, I pull back the sheets and stare at Jackie's slender back and think about trying to juice her up in her sleep and just slide it in. I pull the sheets back further and trace her bare legs with my fingertips. I hover over her bottom and start to lick each golden brown buttock. She whimpers in her sleep and rolls over, squashing my head underneath her midriff. I prise myself out.

I still can't sleep. I get to thinking about Sonia. Now, Sonia loves dick – of this I am sure. She has that slightly impatient look about her, as though she's trying to read your mind, pre-guess whether you're as madly into fucking as she is. It's like she doesn't want to waste too much valuable time with any fags. Sonia. I haven't heard too much noise from next door. I figure that it won't do any harm just to take a look, see if she's still awake.

I creep back out into the front room. Elvis and Sonia are curled up on the sofa, flat out – and fully clothed. I shake her and put my hand over her mouth. Rather than opening her eyes wide and stifling a scream like they do on *Hart To Hart*, she just shakes her hair free and gives me a dirty smile. Her breath is rancid. She disentangles herself from Elvis.

'I'd given up on you,' she teases.

'What happened there, then?'

'He just crashed out.'

'Should've come and joined us two.'

'I would of, but I promised her I wouldn't.'

I feel a little uneasy once I've made sense of this.

'She really likes you, Jackie.'

There's a bit of a silence. Sonia's eyes are burning.

'Shall we find somewhere?' she offers. I lead her through to the tiny kitchen and don't bother to put the light on and, to my considerable surprise as we haven't even kissed, Sonia gets down and starts to suck me. A nosh from the Nosh Queen. She handles my balls while she's sucking, alternating deep draughts which take my entire length inside her with delicate tongue-jobs on my bell. She's a fucking pro and there's no way I'm hanging on for the ride, not after all the messing around with Jackie. I pull out of her mouth and indicate for her to kneel on the floor. Brusquely masturbating her for a moment with three fingers, I push my way in, impatient. I hold her around the waist, thumbs on her spine as she bucks back into me, kicking her heels into my arse and urging me on. I manage to hold on for a respectable duration before I come and come inside her. She seems okay about it. She lies there, getting her breath back, covered in sweat and laughing. I think she's enjoyed it. She seemed to.

'You okay?' I venture.

'Sound, yeah,' she laughs, still breathless. She's watching my cock go down.

'That what you wanted?'

'Yeah.'

'Good.'

She pushes herself up and takes another look at my knob. I suppose it's quite a big one. Bigger than Elvis', for sure.

'Makes a change from the bouncers.'

I feign interest, sensing a put-down just around the next bend.

'They just throw us down and bang us everywhere.'

She pronounces 'throw' as 'trow'.

'Sounds erotic.'

She rolls her eyes.

'Oh, it is, mate.'

'Well, we had to keep it quiet, didn't we?'

'We can go outside if you want. There's a tip just on the corner. No one'll hear us there.'

'You're pure class, Sonia.'

She laughs and holds my stare.

'Come 'ead. That's if you've got another one in you.'

'What about your bezzie, fast asleep next door?'

'Wake her up. She'll be chocker at missing out. She's well into that. Two or three fellas bangin' 'er at a time.'

My face must have dropped several yards.

'Oops!' says Sonia, wickedly. She lifts my chin up with one finger.

'Did she tell you she's a Vicky?'

I nod. Sonia shrieks like a mynah bird.

'The *rip*! And you were having it?'

'Yeah. Why not? That's what she told me.'

'You wouldn't be the first. Says that to all the lads she's cracked on.'

She stands there now, legs astride, looking me up and down.

'Usually the ones who've gorra few bob,' she adds with a wink. She must have twigged that what I need is a little salt rubbing in the wound. I laugh out loud, feeling foolish but quite happy.

'Some mate you are!' I say.

'Shit!' says Sonia, covering her mouth with her hand, the picture of wide-eyed concern. She grins. 'Have I blown it for her, now?'

Sonia and I neck languorously and finger each other and I fuck her from behind standing up in the bathroom, both of us watching in Elvis' brass shaving mirror. She's a beautiful girl, Sonia, but she's mad. She's made for Prince Charles or a Tory politician. She'd blow their minds. But we both know that she'll end up in a maisonette on the Nocky with four kids and a fat, tattooed fella who knocks her around. Maybe I should start seeing her. Why not? I feel sad for her as she throws a blanket over Elvis and gets back under it with him.

Elvis sugars his chocolate and surveys the Lime Street station canteen. John, Marty and Batesy are on one table, arguing about a horse, or something. The Spics, Danny Allen and a few others are sitting around reading newspapers and there are a few in the little offy next to the canteen. All in all it's a very poor showing for our inaugural trip to Blackpool, Christmas or not. Elvis takes the spoon out of his mug and sucks the froth off it.

'Not many here, is there?' he says.

'Oh, Master of Understatement!'

'Knobhead!'

I take ages chewing the last morsel of my sarnie. Danny bounces over, jaunty as ever.

'A'right, boys! No Woody, then, eh?'

Elvis grunts. He's been in a stinking mood since we got up. He barely said ta-ra to the girls. I beckon for Danny to sit down.

'So what's happened then, Dan? This all to do with John and Christy?'

Danny glances nervously over at Godden, anxious that he shouldn't be heard.

'Ah, you know what they're like. Being all Woodchurchist, aren't they? They've all gone on the Ormskirk train. Few of the others've gone with 'em.'

Don't tell me, I think. Baby Millan.

'Baby's gone. Marty says their Damien and Powelly and all the little cunts've gone. Went dead early, this morning. Probably a good little crew, like.'

Elvis looks up suddenly.

'So is it because of The Chelsea, or what? Coz if it is, then these cunts are even sadder than I thought.'

Danny shrugs.

'Dunno, like. Better ask John. I heard that he'd been down the Woody to see Christy and everything's smooth.'

'So it'd seem,' mutters Elvis.

'I know it's only Blackpool an' that, but we should always stick together, wherever we go. Mad, all these splinter groups,' I offer.

'Hey, don't be thinking Blackpool's like Llandudno or something,' warns Danny. 'I know some Everton lads went there in the Cup last year, thought it was going to be a doddle. This is the God's Honest, right. Got legged all round town by about ten thousand of the twats!'

That's all I want to hear. Blackpool were only relegated last season and we've never been there. People tend to assume that seaside towns are going to be a day out, a smirk. We've all been looking forward to Blackpool for ages. Danny seems oblivious to the effect his glad tidings are having on Elvis and me.

'Risky gaff, Blackpool.' He pulls one of his in-the-know faces. 'For real.'

Magnificent. So twenty of us, if that, are getting the ordinary to once sunny, now risky Blackpool where we'll be up against a crew that battered Everton as recently as last year. Danny ups and leaves. Elvis observes my tense fizzog, knowing how nervous I get.

'Spoofer, him, lar! Fucken Blackpool! *Stroll* it!'

Nice but not exceptionally convincing one, Elvis. The conversation turns to Eddie Spark, who's been given six weeks in DC for distributing racist literature. Even with remission, he'll be in over Christmas. Quite fitting, really, and it crosses my mind that the irony wasn't lost on the magistrate. Swelled by late arrivals, there are twenty-seven of us on the 11.33 to Blackpool North. It's an oldish crew and there's quite a good atmos on the train, with Godden regularly calling upon Elvis and me to back up his Stuart Hall story with sound effects and facial expressions where necessary. The journey flies by, but the butterflies return as we file off the train, subdued by the cold Irish Sea winds and unsure when or where the first ambush is going to take place.

Marty tries to get everyone to jump the tram as far as Blackpool Pleasure Beach and walk it from there, but we end up taking the backstreets all the way, stopping just the once for a drink. It's eerily quiet, with no sign of match-day crowds until we're almost upon the stadium. I'm braced for it. As we cross over for the away end, I know that they're going to come pouring out of the sidestreets and pile into us from everywhere. There are so few of us that the last of us are crossing the road as the front few reach the other side. Any second now. My fist is clenched in my pocket and I hope that Elvis has got his Stanley – maybe they'll do a Wrexham. But nothing happens. There really is no one around this end of the ground apart from a couple of taciturn Busies.

'This the away end, mate?' asks Danny.

'Last time I looked.'

My stomach only settles when we're finally at the turnies, paying our one-fifties. Once inside we're greeted by a raggedy mob of Junior Squad and various Woodchurch heads all made up to see us and all talking at once. There's a good crew of them, sixty maybe, though we're dwarfed by this massive covered stand. It's hard to figure out why Blackpool don't use it for their own supporters instead of that poky, unprotected little terrace they flock to. Woollies, eh?

The magnificent sixty have had big trouble before the game and are expecting murder afterwards – hence their unrestrained delight at seeing us lot. There's been a brawl in the square outside Yates' Wine Lodge and, heavily outnumbered, the lads have been on the back foot all the way up to the ground. In classic Tranmere away style, though, they've had the cheek to walk round to the Blackpool end and front them right under the Busies' noses.

'How many of 'em?' demands Marty.

'Couple hundred, tops,' says Baby. He's a sly little cunt but he doesn't spoof. 'They're fuck all, the Blackpool, but they've got the lads off the fair with 'em. Powelly smacked this grock, big fucken meff, really twatted him but would the cunt fuck go down. We all run in on him. It was like King Kong. Busies fucken leathered him good style. Think they hate the gypos more than they hate us.'

With no Christy or Tony present and Hardy so drunk that he'd agree to sort it all out with a game of poker, the Woodchurch heads are soon back on board. I can't wait for full time and barely notice an exhilarating second-half display by Tranmere to peg back a three-goal deficit and come away with a draw. Everyone mobs up at the top of the terracing and as soon as the final whistle goes we pour down the crumbling steps and start heaving at the gates. The Busies signal for the gate stewards to open up. One of them leans over to me.

'You'll be back here in a minute asking to be let back in. We're not puddens, up 'ere, you know!'

But I'm not arsed, now. The Pack rides again. I love it when we're wilding like this, the demon energy driving everyone on and we know absolutely that there isn't a crew to touch us. We get around the corner and start the jog of mayhem. It always makes the mob look bigger when you're moving and I'm sure the extra blood rush makes you do things you'd maybe think twice about, another day.

There's a big crew up ahead. Can't tell yet if it's them or just the bulk of the match crowd, making their way home. John Godden tests the water.

'DZUH! RO! VUZ!'

Everyone's with him. It echoes round the terraced street. We give it again, louder this time and it sounds fearsome. The mob up ahead stops. It's them. I'm breathing hard and ready to go and everyone's looking to Marty and John, but Blackpool come steaming back down the road doing this pathetic Red Indian whooping, obviously expecting us to shit. We hate whooping. Everyone just runs at them. They stop dead in the street, no more than fifty yards up ahead, sad woollies every one, Birmos, Martens, the works.

Laughably, this is a ploy. Another mob comes up round the back of us, this lot not so much whooping as ooh-ooh-oohing. These ones must be the Natives. We all know each other so well and we're so used to offs like this that we don't even glance back at them. We plough straight into the first bunch of divvies and give it right to them. They're running like fuck, the shithouses, jumping over car bonnets and hammering on people's doors, anything to get away. It's a better rush, this, seeing a new mob witness The Pack at close quarters for the first time. You can see it in their faces that they've never come across anything like us, that yellow light of fear and respect in their eyes as they pedal back and run for it.

This one cunt with a ginger Afro and a chipped front tooth steals one on me with a studded glove, but he doesn't hit me true, just glances me and loses his footing in the follow-through. I'm on him in a flash, stamping him back down, kicking him again and again and again in the kite until he goes limp and then I kick him in the side of the head and stamp on his ear and yock on him to let him know he's shit.

The back-up firm can't like what they see, because they disappear as quickly as they arrived on the scene. We can hear some beaut with a dead loud voice rallying them in the streets nearby, so we know it isn't over yet. The way he says 'Blackpool' sounds like he's being sick.

'Come on Beugh-lough-poll! Yoh shit! Yoh getten torn apart in yurrown town!'

Bit of a Manc accent in there somewhere. They'll be back. John, Hardy and Batesy are at the front of our crew with me, Elvis and Marty at the back, everyone very hyper, eyes darting everywhere. We're getting towards central Blackpool and I sense somehow that this is where it's going to go off good style. There's an intensely weird atmos with laden Christmas shoppers bustling off home and flushed Hen Night crews already starting to come out for the night. In the middle of it all, a mob of rogues from Birkenhead trying to make it back to the station and knowing that we'll have to scrap every inch of the way. Something catches my eye behind us and there they are, back again. Clever this time, twos and threes slipping across the road about a hundred yards back, hanging back in the shadows trying to get their numbers up before we suss them and rag them again. I nudge Marty, then out of nowhere this repulsive, retarded-looking skinhead is next to us. He's so tall, about six-seven, that he has to stoop to speak to us. Me and Marty are both over six foot, but this freak is Lurch. Quietly, he reasons with Marty:

'Come on, Scouse. You're the boss, eh? You and me go for a little walk. Just down there, like. Just two of us. Want to do it here? Come on, then. 'It me. You 'ave first whack.'

This is silly, playground tough-guy talk and I've got no fears for Marty, but he seems hesitant to give this prick a hiding. I scrutinise the caveman's horrid black V-neck jumper, tufts of chest hair sticking out underneath – in December. I'm just looking at his combat kecks and the dumb-fuck string of spittle dangling from his top lip and I'm just about to smack him myself when Marty crosses the road. I can't believe it. He's shit. From this goon! I stand there, fronting him, staring at the borstal tatt on his cheek when, no backlift or anything, he bangs me into the middle of the street with a huge uppercut. Stunned, I try to sit up and I see Elvis hurl himself on the grock and sink his teeth into his cheek and I see Baby flash a blade across him and I hear wild screaming from Bigskin and then I pass out. When I come round, only a little while later, Damien O'Connor is supporting me next to some car park wall and pointing down the street, hysterical.

'Look at that, lar! See that! Fucken caned them! Legging the twats back into last fucken week!'

The familiar distant sound of The Pack chasing down Blackpool's scattering mob is supplemented by sirens. My jaw aches like mad. I touch it and wince. Could be broken. Everyone starts to filter back, eager to avoid the escort and conscious that the last train to Liverpool is at half-six. They gather round me, jabbering about their heroics and exaggerating their own part in it. It starts to dawn on me that I'm not getting the attention my plucky display deserves. I stood up while Marty shit his kecks and now it seems that I'm the one embarrassment who got whacked. Elvis comes over, out of breath, grinning through a bleeding lip.

'Took one there, didn't you? Fuckenell! You alright?'

I wince self-deprecatingly. I can't exactly call Marty a shite hawk so I keep mum and think of how I can let the truth be known. Not that Marty lost it, so much, but that I wasn't the mug out there. He comes over.

'Fuckenell, Carty, lar! Won't be getting in the way of one of those again in a hurry, eh, mate?'

This is just what I need.

'I took it for you, Mart,' I grin. 'Wanted to prove me loyalty, an' 'at. Earn me colours.'

Everyone laughs. Marty is determined to get his viewpoint across.

'Couldn't fucken believe yeah. I picks a little spot for me and the grock to go and do it. Not some shady fucken backstreet where he's got all his standoffs lined up – somewhere we can all see what's going on. Next minute I looks up and there's The Prof stickin 'is chin out going, come 'ead mate, have a swipe!'

This version of events casts me in a goodish light, though again I'm not happy about this re-emergence of The Prof. I finally buried that last season when I leathered three Forest fans at Crewe station on the way back from Walsall. And I can't convince myself that Marty was really going to have a go with Bigskin. I've never known Marty to back down from anyone, and we've certainly been in worse situations than today – but we've usually had a good drink, too. I know Marty's no bullshitter – just that I was closest to him and I had the distinct impression that he dropped his load. He's probably convinced himself he was going to do it right. I'll never know for sure.

The trip home is a scream. We change at Preston and board the Glasgow to Liverpool just as PNE's hordes are returning from Huddersfield. For once, I'm glad that we miss the fray. I'm fucked and my jaw, though not broken, aches badly. We take over the buffet after terrorising the lone steward. Everyone's drinking Scotch, rum and vodka compliments of British Rail. A couple of Busies get on at St Helen's but, knowing that the steward would phone ahead for assistance, the evidence, in the form of a dozen empty bottles, has already been gleefully lashed at a gang of Soul Boys at Wigan. As we approach Lime Street, Baby tells me that his sister wants to see me again. I look at him, dumbfounded. I met her last week, he tells me. Her name's Lilly. I start to stutter an explanation but he winks and pats me on the shoulder.

'Whatever, man. Just passing on the message.'

We pile off at Liverpool, triumphant, knackered and completely pissed, and everyone walks down Lime Street as far as The Big House, singing:

'Don't be mistaken and don't be misled,
We are not Scousers, we're from Birkenhead.
You can fuck your cathedrals and your pierhead,
We are not Scousers, we're from Birkenhead.'

But there's no takers.

8 December 1979

Elvis has been very low lately, but right now he's making me feel suicidal. We're having a quiet drink in The Letters, listening to Clock DVA on the jukey and not saying much. You wouldn't think it's Christmas. Just down the road, the united might of the Birkenhead Civil Services are holding their annual Chrimbo bash at Alfresco's. Even now, early as it is, besozzled middle-management types will be closing in on the unfortunate little darling from the office they've had their eye on all year. There's one or two from the Land Registry who drink in The Copperfield who I wouldn't mind getting to know, but the mood Elvis is in it looks like I'll be spending the evening coaxing him down from the bridge. I only asked him along because it's Halifax tomorrow and I'm staying at his. He drags his hair out of his eyes dramatically.

'I dunno, you know.'

He looks at me for some kind of reaction.

'I just don't know. We're the Rubaiyat, aren't we?'

I clear my throat. We've been smoking More. We think More are a groovy-looking cigarette and, as smoking is obligatory at this time of year, their menthol-flavoured cheroot has been favoured with our custom.

'Know watcha mean, El.'

He looks at me like I'm patronising him but, in spite of Elvis' dogged attempts to spoil the party before it's even started, I do have some sympathy with his current ennui.

'I do!'

Elvis nods his acceptance of this new and slightly more

impassioned bid and exhales mint-flavoured smoke all over me.

'Dunno, Carty, lar. May just do one. Get a little flat in Sefton Park. London, even.'

He peers up from under his fringe and blows it out of his eyes.

'Got to do *something*. Doin' me swede in, all this.'

For all that Elvis and I are so tight, I don't actually know him too well. We do a lot of things together, but we talk with an unspoken understanding that there're barriers we won't cross. So I'm guessing when I say he's a dealer. Probably small-time, probably just pot and speed. I don't think he's a robber. He's never short of cash for someone who, to my knowledge, has never broken sweat in a paddy-field, but I've never felt any great need to come out and ask him what he does and the longer it's gone on the more I quite like not knowing. He's just the same. Even when Mum died he just sort of acted like it wasn't happening. Made no direct reference to it at all. I think I appreciated that. Now he's sitting here, telling me that he's on the point of vanishing out of my life forever, and I don't know for sure that he's ever had a girlfriend or how many brothers and sisters he has. I know he's the eldest, I know his dad's dead and I know he left the Ford when he was sixteen. Whatever, though, I have to agree with him. We're both going to the same place. Nowhere.

Alfresco's is swinging. Spanning the far wall is a trestle-table, overflowing with unwanted food. Underneath the table couples writhe self-consciously, trying to be the talk of the office tomorrow.

'*Da summerollidee an' da Christmas piss-up.*'

He's right, as usual, old Bob. And he's not here. He's out of hospital now, back home convalescing from what the specialist advised him was not a heart-attack but nervous exhaustion. Bob McNally. The most focused, stable man I know, smashed by a nervous breakdown at the age of forty-three. I survey the range of curled-up sandwiches and trifles whose hardening custard skins have been violated by cigarette-butts, and gingerly pick out a selection of turkey cuts and doughy macaroni. Everything tastes of nothing.

Elvis is at the bar talking to a DHSS punk. She's a bit of a Siouxsie wannabee – if Siouxsie wanted to be fifteen stone. She's got the mad black eye make-up, masses of dyed black hair and blue lipstick, but she's not wholly unattractive. The enormous bust is tressed up in a velvet bodice and prominently displayed in the shop window. Sitting on the stool next to them, facing away from the bar and staring, bored, into the middle-distance is a gum-chewing gargoyle who I presume to be her mate. Her plump head is completely shaven and she's wearing a ripped Ronnie Biggs T-shirt and the most inappropriately short kilt I've ever seen. She looks like Divine. I *have* to shag her. I sidle up to the bar and order a pint of lager, turn to Divine and say:

'Hi! What you having?'

She looks me up and down with unadulterated contempt, gets up off her stool and marches off, fatly, leaving me to watch the office girls and boys at play. Some of the worst dancing I have ever seen, anywhere, unfolds before me. Orchestral Manoeuvres have become so popular that even the Land Reg. pricks are flinging themselves around to 'Electricity', knees and elbows colliding, faces set in ecstatic good-time grins, heads being tossed in risible approximations of 'modern' dancing. I'm desperate to be up there with them, with Divine as my dancing partner, but even she doesn't want to know. A nice-looking blonde stands next to me, waiting to get served, and I catch her giving me the eye in the mirror. She's familiar but I can't place her. What the hell. I start wiggling my eyebrows at her in the mirror, to make her laugh. I make her laugh.

'You're Paul Carty, aren't you?'

'That, madam, I am,' I say and kiss her hand. She giggles. 'And you are?'

'You won't remember me. I was at the Girls' School when you got expelled.'

'I was not expelled. I left.'

'Sorry. All the girls said you'd been expelled for stabbing a teacher.'

'I think I would've been jailed for stabbing a teacher, let alone expelled.'

'Sorry.'

'Stop apologising and tell me your name.'

'Annabel Stiles. I was in the year above your crowd.'

'I got the bus with them. I didn't knock around with them.'

'Sorry.'

She puts her hand over her mouth and giggles. She really is very pretty. I can't make out whether she's a little bit innocent or she's one of those randy pony-club types from Gayton. Her dress code suggests that her mum still has a say in her wardrobe – a taffeta gown doesn't seem quite the thing for the Civil Service hoolie. What's for sure, though, is that she's very nice and there's nothing to be lost in talking to her. I turn sideways to give her my fullest attention.

'So what *really* happened then?'

'School?'

'Mmm . . .'

Her eyes open wide as if she's expecting some gruesome confession about opium or homosexuality. A tactic I haven't used for some time presents itself. When Mum was first diagnosed as having cancer and, especially, after she died, I passed myself off to vulnerable girls as a withdrawn, tragic, introspective figure who was somehow beyond the trivialities of teenage kicks and touched by a deep and melancholy mysticism. I was the sensitive guy. They fell for it every time. If I wasn't getting enough attention at parties I'd just go and stand by a window, gazing out into nothing. Without fail, some heavenly creature would come over and ask me what's up. I'd pretend that they'd jolted me out of a not unpleasant reverie.

'Oh . . . nothing,' I'd say with a thin smile. Then we'd sit down and I'd tell them, in horrific detail, how I'd seen my beautiful mother wither away in front of me in a matter of months. The girls would nod, stricken, unsure what to say.

'Somehow, when you've been through that, these kids parties seem . . . It's difficult to connect with people . . .'

I was brilliant at acting confused and leaving sentences hanging in the air. For a variety of reasons, the girls were unanimously willing to sacrifice their flesh upon the altar of my suffering. Annabel Stiles must not have run with the racy crowd, or she'd already know all this. The truth is, one term into my A-levels Mum was confirmed as having cancer and I *did* suddenly fail to see the relevance of two more years at school. So I left. That was it. I just stopped going.

'I just stopped going.'

'Why?'

'It just seems so futile to be going to school when your mum's dying of cancer.'

Even now, I love the recoil when they twig the depth of your situation.

'I'm sorry . . . I mean . . . shit! Paul, I had no idea. God.'

She turns and runs towards the toilets. Fuck! Too much! Far too graphic for a nice girl like Annabel. Damn. I wonder whether I should go after her. Fuck it. Everyone's pairing off. I decide to find Elvis and call it a night. Then I see her. Sitting demurely at the little cocktail bar at the other end of the restaurant is Suzy. I don't think she's seen me. The plan comes to me in a flash.

I'm quite prepared to bide my time, keep an eye on her from a distance. She keeps on checking her watch. Probably won't be staying long. I'm surprised to see her here at all. Maybe she's after somebody. Whatever, I can't afford to take my eyes off her. I start to enjoy watching her. She's a graceful, beautiful woman with the most alluring way of holding herself. She's full of poise – aloof, yet giving a sense of vulnerability. I could watch her all night but, after sparking up a black Sobranie, she scoops up her bag, slides off her stool and she's gone. I'm after her immediately but she's completely vanished. The pushbars of the Emergency Exit have been opened so I dart after her, but all that's out there is a very young C.A. being sick. Shit! I've lost *her* too! I turn to go back in when a car beeps tinnily and flashes its headlights. I strain my eyes to make out a 2CV parked by The Birkenhead News and cautiously make my way towards it. The window goes down. It's Suzy, trying to look mysterious.

'Looking for anyone in particular,' she teases. I say nothing and try to smoulder back at her. She holds my gaze. She leans across and opens the passenger door. So *I'm* the fucking quarry. Suddenly, I'm not so sure I fancy another of Suzy's weird fucking games. I do not feel in command. I shoot her a nasty look, shake my head and go back inside.

I find Divine, gassed on Red Witches, and coax her into a slowie. Lionel Ritchie doesn't know how right he is when he mentions that she's three times a lady. I can't get my hands to meet behind her back. She manhandles my testicles and slobbers on my neck. It's looking good for a shag.

9 December 1979

'NICE COCK!!'

By now the whole train is shouting it. Hardy and Baby spent yesterday afternoon in The Eros cinema watching one of the higher art forms, a double-bill of German blueys called *Grunt* and *The Fishmonger*. Still in fits every time they tell us about it, the two of them have been giving us a run-down of the unambiguous dialogue of *Grunt*.

'Mmm . . . good dick!'

'You want me to stick that in your pussy?'

'Mmmm . . . I want all of that baby inside me.'

'Yeah?'

'Yeah!'

'You want me to put my cock inside you?'

On cue, the travelling band of players and storytellers jump up, produce penises of varying dimensions and shout:

'NICE COCK!!'

It was hilarious at first, but now it's getting on my nerves. Typical of Tranmere to milk a good joke to death. I try to change the subject by shouting across at Elvis, who's staring blankly out at the countryside from his window seat on coach C of the Transpennine Sprinter. Even now I don't feel fully comfortable about launching a piss-take on the El, but what the heck.

'So El, you going to tell us what all the crying was about, last night?'

Elvis gives me a filthy glare, but it's too late. The lads are on to it.

'What's all this, El? You been scaring little girls again?'

'Don't think you could call 'em little, Babe. Not with the best will in the world.'

Elvis gamely tells how we brought the two hefty punkettes back to his flat. He calls them Bald Skate and Siouxsie Skate.

'So I'm there, like, in bed with Siouxsie Skate and, like, there's *loads* of her. She's spread out all over me bed. I don't know what bit of her to get into first. And, like, her tits smell of eggs. Great big dirty groodies, they are. Big fuck-off stretch marks right down the sides of 'em . . .'

'Stop it, Elv, I'm getting a hard-on!'

'NICE COCK!!'

'So, er, the crying, Elvis. Why was she crying?'

'Must've been the innate beauty of the occasion. The poetry of me technique must've sort of got to her.'

He's besieged by screwed-up ciggie packets and empty cans.

'Fucken Carty put me off me stroke! It's bad enough trying to get yourself in the mood to pork some piece of blubber without that cunt doing his Christy routine next door! What were you doing to her? Garotting her?!'

It's true to say I gave Divine a perfunctory and brutal going over. A real hate shag. She fucking loved it as well. Relishing my part in this leftish encounter, I sit back as Elvis entertains the train with a faithful imitation of Divine's sound effects:

'Ooh!!Godgodgod-yesyesyes-fuckfuckfuck-cockcockcock!!'

'NICE COCK!!'

'Next one to say nice cock gets a hundred lines!'

'So basically, Elvis, Carty gives the bald skate what for while the other poor bitch is crying cos you can't get a hard-on?'

Elvis thinks about this.

'It's one of them, like. You're trying to imagine you're porkin' Debbie Harry – then you look down and it's Hattie Jacques . . .'

'PHWOOAR!! Class fanny!!'

'I just felt meself go soft inside her. And that was that.'

Once again he's bombarded with litter. Christy and Tony

are back and, while John Godden isn't exactly courting their company, the atmos is fine. Surreally, the train creaks into Bradford Interchange station, then backs out again, going back the way we've just come. Fortunately Batesy is on hand with an explanation.

'See, Halifax sits so deep in the falley that the incline'd be too accute for a normal-bore wail twack, so the twain has to switch twack and appwoach Halifax from like a different angle which is how come we go backwards out of Bwadford. So that the sidings can make the switch.'

We stare at him, dumbstruck. Nobody says a word until Marty breaks the silence.

'That's fascinating, Batesy. Isn't it boys? Absolutely fascinating.'

Everyone laughs and buries Batesy under a volley of knuckles. We've got a fuck of a good crew today, partly with it being the Cup but also because word of The Pack's awaydays is finally starting to spread. A lot of urchins from places like Moreton and Leasowe, who are traditionally at war with Woodchurch and the Ford, have been feeling the backlash of the Liverpool-Birkenhead thing from the Scousers. Even if they support Liverpool or Everton, they're getting hopped on at Moorfields and Limey after the match and a lot of the younger ones are starting to come to Tranmere instead.

Three or four tower blocks are visible as we approach Halifax. Tower blocks are a good measure of how hard a town is going to be. The proliferation of silent towers outside of Doncaster, for example, serves eloquent notice that you're in for a rough afternoon with aggro-crazy Yorkshire in-breds. Northampton, too, stuck in the middle of middle England with its stark concrete skyscrapers, is a place you know you're going to get a row. There is, really, fuck all else to do in places like that. But for all that the towers are a handy indicator, they're not the Holy Bible. Chester flatters to deceive, with the walkways and balconies of Newtown the first thing you see as you come out of the station. Yet aways don't come much easier than Chester. By the same token, for all that Halifax's skyline isn't overly dominated by watchful tenements, we know that there are nutty outlying estates like Mixenden where three-eyed subbies eat their kids and scrap each other all day to pass time.

We trot out of Halifax station, all the Juniors up front, as usual. The initial surge lasts all of a minute, damped down immediately by the cold, persistent drizzle and the complete lack of any Halifax heads. These new gold Lois jumbos of mine are giving me murder, cutting into my hips and gut. I could've got my proper size, a 30 waist, but they were a little loose, didn't quite show my arse to best effect, so I struggled into the 28 and convinced myself they were fine. It's not as though skintight jeans are that fashionable any more, either. I've seen quite a few Odgies in The Apple wearing these weird Inega Carpenter's Jeans which are tight round the ankle and baggy in the leg. Sexy Rexy's is about the only place I've seen them, but I'm not sure about that whole look, gussetted pumps and stripey tops and all that. It's a bit *too* silly. Sexy Rexy's is a hoot, though. They're right onto the scally one-upmanship of the Liverpool fashion scene. Few weeks ago they had these vicious yellow Razzy in the window, with a sign on saying: 'In for 1 week only!' Next to it was another sign saying: 'Why go cold? Free three-star jumper with every Lois purchase!' It'll all end in tears.

I undo the top button of my cords to give me some relief and jog up the hill after the crew. It must be shite supporting Liverpool or Everton, having to stay one step ahead of Chelsea and Arsenal and Man. U. We don't have so much trouble looking better than Scunny.

Or Halifax. There's a dozen lads at the top of this steep road through a dead part of town. I don't know how many Tranmere they were expecting for a Cup game, but our crew is clearly a shock to them. They stand in awe for a moment, as though it's the Romans coming, then leg it back towards the town centre. Marty turns to us. Some of The Pack – me, Hardy, Danny, loads – are falling behind the rest. It's starting to slat down – cold, freezing fucking rain.

'COME 'EAD!!' he bellows. Maybe he's still embarrassed about Blackpool. 'THEY'RE UP THERE!! THEY'RE UP THERE!! LET'S GET INTO THEM!!'

We shuffle halfheartedly to close up the gap. I don't feel like this at all. The waistband of my kecks is rubbing into my flesh and the rain is Yorkshire's own hell. There's something else, though, something gnawing away inside, unsettling me, telling me I don't want to be here. I try to track back through everything that's been done and said in the past twenty-four hours, but I can't put my finger on anything.

'COME 'EAD!!'

Marty. He's part of the problem. I've always wanted him to know that I'm not a knobhead, I'm worth my place. I suppose I overdo it a bit sometimes, over-extend myself. I'll always grab the chance to talk to him but he doesn't give much away. After everyone settled down on the train I spent a good half-hour just chatting to him – a privilege, indeed. He spoke in bursts, not looking at me but fiddling with a KitKat wrapper, staring out of the window, about how all the ordinary people who voted for Thatcher are already starting to get it in the arse. We got onto the subject of Trades Unions. He's a shop steward at Cadbury's in Moreton, though he's not exactly a powerful advocate.

'T&G, lar, talk about sheep in wolves' clothing. Fucken toothless. Our goons want it all custy with the management just like they always have done. Laissez faire cunts.'

Some fella. For half an hour he's a demagogue with his laconic but passionate slant on real life, life as it's lived, the hopes and dreams of the hopeless. It's like he got off the train and got into a different suit of armour. I've never felt easy around him. He's got a good line in making me, personally, feel very insignificant, and right now I'm not sure I need his brand of reality.

'I'm fucked, lar,' I say to Danny Allen. It's not a total spoof either. I've noticed lately that I get out of breath far too easily. The hill has done for me.

'Done yourself in pounding that skate,' laughs Danny.

'Something like that.'

We're approaching a pub, The Rose and Crown, on the periphery of central Halifax, which at least shows signs of life. There's lights on inside. The Pack has slowed up. There's no sign of any Halifax mob. For once I speak out of turn.

'Come 'ead!' I shout, stopping by the pub. 'We're gonna fucken shrink walking round this yard in the rain. I've got a delicate chest. I need whisky!'

I go into the pub. I'm stupidly flattered when a goodly crew follow me inside, Marty included. Godden takes a little crew on the mooch including, to my real surprise, a suddenly hyperactive Elvis. Christy goes with them, too. Whatever will they think of next? The Junior Squad head off on their customary robbing spree while the bulk of our contingent settle down to the heady business of pool-playing, crisp-munching and bullshit-talking. Batesy puts The Police on the jukey. I'm strangely cheered by this.

Ten minutes later, Elvis is back on his own, barely able to draw breath. 'You've got to come and see this!! You won't believe it, lar!'

Try as we do, we can't get any sense out of Elvis, who is close to hysteria, other than the words 'Doctor Who, lar!' He collapses on the floor and screws his face up in comic agony as silent, racking laughter jolts his skinny body. Batesy kicks him clumsily but good-naturedly. It does the trick. Elvis manages, momentarily, to pull himself together. He tugs me by the sleeve.

'Just come and see this, Carty, lar. You'll piss yourself. Come 'ead.'

Most of the lads ignore him and carry on with their wondrous stories, but a decent crew of us drink up and head off into Halifax. Elvis, starting to giggle again as we enter a cobbled sidestreet, takes us to a posh-looking hotel, The St James. A colourful sandwich-board stands at the bottom of the steps. It says: Saturday 9th December. Seventh International Doctor Who Convention. Elvis cracks up.

'Whaddidifuckentellyah!! Hahahahah!! Fucken better or what?'

'Er . . . yeah!'

'What d'you mean yeah?'

'Sound. Doctor Who an' that. Nice one.'

'He's fucken in there!'

'Who is?'

'Doctor Who!!'

Now it's our turn to start laughing.

'Come 'ead Elvis,' says Marty, holding out his hand. 'Hand over the acid!'

Elvis grabs me by the sleeve again and pulls me up the steps and through the hotel's revolving door. I signal for the others to follow. An obliging porter who looks like Benny Hill, steps forward.

'This rest of party, sir?' he asks. God knows what bullshit Elvis has been feeding him.

'Aye, mate, this is us. Fourth Bramley Dr Who Appreciation Society.'

We're too stunned to say anything. Elvis slips Benny a pound note and he leads all twenty of us up a single flight of deep purple stairs and nods to a, frankly, hideous woman behind a makeshift desk who's collecting tickets.

'Bramley party, Alma. Pee eye ay.'

She studies her list.

'Have they? I've not gottum down here . . .'

Benny winks at Elvis. The old pro.

'Got account with hotel. Paid through company.'

This seems to satisfy Alma who waves us through, giving Marty a frightening leer as he passes by.

'Later, love,' he growls. Charmer. 'How much to pork the horror?' he whispers to me.

'Me or you,' I chuckle. Lads. But I'm starting to feel more perky.

Elvis runs ahead, keen to show off his find, his shoulders already shuddering with the latest attack of the humours. Inside the function room are approximately one hundred people, all bar one or two dressed as Doctor Who. They stand around in threes and fours, just as casual as you like, nibbling at plates of sandwiches and swapping, no doubt, the latest Dr Who trivia. It's safely one of the queerest things I've ever seen.

I'm horrified to spy Marty, engaged in conversation with an enormous red-faced man whose Doctor garb is topped off with an impressive white stetson hat. God forbid that O'Connor should be getting shirty with the Texas Branch. Still mindful of Stuart Hall, I hurry to mediate.

'Yeah, it's the God's honest truth, man. Jon Pertwee played mandolin on "Strawberry Fields Forever". Didn't he, Carty?'

'Was it the mandolin or the harp?'

The large American is wide-eyed as he scribbles all this sensational news down on the back of a paper doily.

'Say, what's your name again, sir?'

'Marty. Marty O'Connor.'

They shake.

'Marty. I'm John but you can call me Stew.'

'Don't tell me! John Stewart, right?'

'Er, wrong, but hey! Don't let that stop you! Listen, Mack.'

'Marty.'

'How'd you like to come to Austin, Texas, as guest of the Texas Chapter of the Society, and speak to the brethren about this startling new evidence regarding the early activities of Jon Pertwee? We'd cover all your expenses, naturally, and I feel sure that we take care of, ah, other emoluments, too. What d'you say?'

The fat guy wiggles his eyebrows lasciviously in a 'tempted, huh?' sort of way. Marty pretends to think about it, then breaks into a huge grin.

'I say, when do I start! Stew!' and thrusts out his hand. Stew ignores it and crushes Marty's substantial frame in a suffocating bearhug. He releases him just as he's about to expire and scribbles something on a business card.

'I'm back in Austin Friday. Going to London, England and Dublin, Ireland en route, so maybe leave it a week. But gimme a call, Mack. It's been awesome having you.'

'Same here, Stew. Same here.'

They hug like old beer buddies. Stew slots the card into Marty's top pocket and lumbers off in search of more interesting Whodees. I wag my finger at Marty.

'Not the act of an international socialist, Mr O'Connor.'

'You what? Cunt's probably got 2,000 square miles of prime oil country that his grandaddy stole from the Mexicans and I'm supposed to feel bad about nabbing a free trip? He should give me a fucken job!'

I shake my head in mock despair but, while I wouldn't greet a brother from overseas with anything other than servile helpfulness, I'm quite tickled by Marty's exchange with Stew. We cast our eyes around for the others. Marty grins and nudges me. Perched ludicrously atop an overly-tall bar stool is Elvis. He is lost in conversation with Tom Baker. I roll my eyes at Marty.

'What the fuck's he saying to *him*?'

'Probably trying to get him to come the match.'

I laugh out loud at the prospect. Touchingly, Marty's encouraged sufficiently by my tittering to have another bash at this being-a-wag lark.

'Be the first crew to go away by Tardis.'

This time it's an effort to grind a smile out, so I indicate that we should join Elvis and his new mate. As we get close, I can hear Elvis' insistent voice haranguing Mr Baker.

'Just think about it, Tom. Don't dismiss it. It'd bring science back within the grasp of the common man. You'd be a hero!'

Tom Baker is in fits of laughter.

'I just don't know if the common man is ready to see Doctor Who in that sort of light!'

Elvis is laughing, too, knowing he's beat but still pushing it.

'Why not, Tom? The Doctor's a scientist. Right?'

'Correct. Ish.'

'And this is, like, an experiment?'

Again, Tom Baker roars with infectious laughter.

'Pass. Want a drink?'

Elvis smiles and shrugs in defeat and asks for a vodka and PLJ. Little twat! Robbing my drink to impress the Doctor! Marty and I step forward. It feels perfectly proper to be stood here, at a bar in a hotel in Halifax, chewing the fat with Tom Baker.

'These are me mates, Tom. Paul and, er, Martin. They're big fans.'

Tom shakes hands and offers us a drink. I'm dying for one, but decline. Marty orders a double Jamieson's.

'Your very amusing chum here has been trying to persuade the Doctor to take a Living Science Roadshow out to the provinces.'

I pull a 'He's mad, Elvis!' sort of face. Marty gets in between me and Tom.

'What's he up to, Doc? What's his game? If he needs a slap, just let me know!'

Tom Baker looks down at his drink.

'Hah! No, I think not. It's even more basic than that. Young, er, Elvis, here, is trying to impress upon me the scientific and cultural value that could be brought to society at large if the Doctor were to travel the land, er . . . Elvis?'

'Lighting his farts! It'd be a smash!'

Tom Baker and I guffaw generously at this, but Marty stays silent. He's just waiting for a pause, so that he can jump in again.

'Funnily enough, Tom, I've been invited to the Austin convention as a special guest. I'm a bit of a specialist on early *Doctor Who* and, er, Stew's into all the early stuff, too and he's invited me over to lecture . . .'

'Stew?'

Marty desparately looks around for the big Texan, then remembers the business card. He whips it out and hands it to Tom. Doctor Who looks at it and smiles and reads it out loud. *'Stew Pidd – Credulous Yank. I'll believe any old bull y'all tell me. Have a nice day!'*

Before I can stop it I'm screeching like a parakeet, but fortunately Elvis and Tom are laughing, too. For the first time, ever, I see Marty redden and flail for words. He looks bloody ridiculous.

'Maybe I'll see you there, Martin!' says Tom, and touching the rim of his big felt hat, he goes to leave. He stops a couple of yards ahead of Elvis, lifts one leg, flicks his Zippo and lets rip a turbulent fart which bursts briefly into corruscating flash-flame, then strolls off without turning round. Nice one, Doctor. There's a kerfuffle from the other side of the room. Doctor Who lookalikes are bumping into each other and tripping over and, one or two of them, strangling themselves on their scarves. Danny and Hardy come over, sniggering.

'Look at that, lar,' laughs Hardy.

'All our own handiwork!' proclaims Danny. 'Tied all their fucken scarves together. Fucken mayhem!'

The bloody headcase. He's a menace to society, that Danny Allen.

'Time we were off, anyway,' says Marty, looking at his watch. I preguess him.

'Mart. Don't go looking for Mr Pidd, eh?'

His ears redden slightly, but he forces a smile.

'I can take a joke, can't I?'

Nobody says anything. We thank the fantastically ill–made Alma profusely and skip down the stairs, out through the revolving doors and into bedlam. Backs to us, mobbed up on the corner of the cobbled street but retreating slowly as bricks and glasses and lumps of stone land all around them, is Halifax's crew. We're not even all out of the St James. Halifax haven't seen us.

'Come 'ead, Carty. Steal this on 'em.'

My stomach tightens. My heart is going thumping mad. I can barely breathe. My palate dries up and my throat is bitter with bile. Up ahead I can now see Billy Powell, Christy, Baby and loads of the lads advancing warily on Halifax's firm. They look mental. Billy spots Marty and says something to the others. This seems to give them the lift they need. They come running down this pedestrianised bit and Halifax turn on their heels and leg it. Marty and Batesy run in, screaming jibberish. Me and Elvis and the others follow, trying to cut Halifax off before they can get up the sidestreet ahead. We get a few wild kicks in, slam a few of them up against shop windows but they manage to get up into this big shopping street and disappear. Batesy gives chase with Tony Byatt, just to see where they've gone. Billy comes over, looking grim. He comes straight up to Marty. He looks like he's going to cry.

'Your Damien's been carted off in an ambulance,' says Billy, fudging it.

Marty doesn't say anything, so I ask all the questions.

'What's happened?'

'Some grock pulled a blade on him.'

'Is he bad?'

'Dunno. Think he got it in the side. Could've gone anywhere.'

Christy jogs over, looking grave.

'You better get back over here take a look at John. I think he's been knifed 'n' all. Fucken blood all over him.'

Marty just stands rooted to the spot. I go with Christy. Danny hesitates, then follows.

'What's been going on, Christy, lar?'

'Fuck knows. We've had little crews all over town, but their mob got into the Juniors, like. Thought they was our main mob. Powelly come back and found John and that, but there just wasn't enough of us.'

'That crew was fuck all! You coulda done them!'

'There's a few primates there, lar. They know how to have a go. Tooled up 'n' all, loads of blades.'

I shake my head gravely. Our rep is finally starting to precede us. Godden is sitting in the doorway of a bookmaker's, clutching his side, his face cramped in agony. He tries to wave me away but I kneel down and feel his forehead and manage to unzip his Peter Storm and get his jumper up. His hand is pushed into his side and he's sucking his breath in in little gasps. There's a lot of blood, but you can see that its source is a small black wound just below his ribcage. The blade must've been fucking thin, a stiletto or something similar. Nasty. Whatever, Godden should've been in hospital ten minutes ago.

'Danny, lar – can you do us a massive favour? I know you're gonna want to go and find these cunts and give it to them like we all do, but someone's got to get John to hozzy. Tell me to fuck off, like, but – will you?'

You could hoist a fleet of Zeppelins on his relief. He pats me on the shoulder.

'No problem, lar. I'll stick with him.'

He jogs off in search of a callbox. Godden's eyelids are flickering alarmingly. His face is deadly white. Batesy returns, walking briskly and full of self-importance.

'Up in the square. By the bus station. Big alehouse.'

Everyone is now standing a respectful few yards away, glancing over at me and Godden, nervously. Marty is still rooted to the spot, looking at the floor. Danny comes sprinting back.

'All in hand. Couple of minutes.'

I thank him and go over to Marty.

'What d'you want to do then, Mart?'

'Our Damien. He's only a little tithead. No threat to no one.'

'That's probably why they went for him. You know what these beasts are like. Subbies. We've got to do this, Marty. We've got to give these woollies a hiding they'll never forget. Come 'ead. For Damien.'

Marty gives me a chilling, neutering look that only an alien could dredge from the pits of its black soul. I have just seen hatred.

'Do one, you. You don't know what you're talking about.'

He turns briefly to the mob.

'Let's go,' he says, quietly. In spite of myself, the adrenalin courses through me. I'll do anything for him.

The cobbled streets of Halifax are dark and shiny in the December rain. We follow Batesy to a big, busy square which seems to double as the bus terminus and the spiritual heart of town. There's loads of people larking around and I don't think Marty's in a mood to discriminate.

There's a big pub in the corner of the square. As we get within striking distance, Batesy, unable to keep a lid on his aggression, tries to get a chant going. Marty turns sharply and signals softly-softly. A little gang of Pakis take a foolish amount of time trudging out of the way, letting it be known that they don't move for any trash in this town. They're quickly and quietly despatched. Three of them are left on the deck. An old lady is spat at by their mates as she comes to offer help.

Outside the pub, two little standoffs are having a laugh with the local scrubbers. So intoxicated are they by the wenches' large and available breasts that they fail to see us coming. Marty strides up to the bigger of the two, picks him up off his feet and launches him sideways through the main window of the pub. The girls scream and run at Marty, lashing out with nails. He bangs the first one under the chin. She's out cold. The others give it toes with the second standoff. These lasses are quality. They'll be frigging themselves for weeks about the hard Scousers who came into town, battered their lads and took the place.

Credit to Halifax, they don't come pouring out of the boozer like knobheads. They come out slowly and walk towards us, business-style with six or seven big ouncer-types at the front, big baldy cunts with muzzies and shrunken Wrangler jackets. But it wouldn't have mattered if there was six or seven hundred of them, they don't stand a chance. I can't resist a horrible smile as one of their main men, who looks like Freddie Mercury, actually gulps hard, like they do in comics. He tries to get himself going, screams at Halifax to get into us, but he knows he's on his last cigarette. Marty runs in and whacks him, spreading his nose and sending the poor grock staggering backwards. We're off. I look for someone to give it to. There's a skinny prick with a perm who looks like the fella from *Kes* on hunger strike. This beaut has been jumping up and down outside the pub like he really wants to know and it's just a question of how many of us he kills. He'll do. I see him knocking over women and children to get away. I go after him but lose him in the mêlée. The Pack are going mental. Billy Powell, who I had down as a principled sort, picks up a dagger-sized shard of glass and buries it in a lad's cheek. I suppose he *is* Damien's bezzy. The lad just wanders round in a little circle, stunned, whimpering. Billy won't leave it at that. He's taking his time and with shocking calm he's aiming kicks at the lad's sides and punching him on the back of his confused, cowering head. It's going off all over the square. Halifax have been scattered. They've offered nothing, they're just running, everywhere, back into the pub, onto buses, into shops. I spot Kes again with two of his mates, trying to walk away as though they've had nothing to do with all this. All they need to do now is whistle innocently. I tap Billy and point at them.

'Come 'ead! These haven't had it!'

Elvis and Batesy see us go after them and catch us up. The three Halifax teds suss that we're on them, and jerk into a frantic Billy Whizz break for the border. They turn into a sidestreet. We've lost them, but we follow, just to make sure. We turn into the same street. It's a dead end, but the other three are still running like fuck. There's only a pub at the end of the courtyard. We smirk at each other. We stop running and walk towards them, relishing the moment. They're banging like fuck on the doors and windows of this pub. I can hear 'A Message To You Rudi' throbbing from inside. No one opens up. They turn, backs flattened up against the pub doors, to face the music. I go for permhead. I give a little hop and flick him in the balls. He's not going to fight. He just wants to get it over with. He doubles and holds his balls. I hammer him in the nape and, just for a second, I'm worried at the noises coming out of him, a sort of gagging, choking for breath. I stand off him. I can hear his mates screaming behind me, pleading with the others to lay off them. It occurs to me that any one of them could've been the twat who did Damien. I'm just shaping up to give him a bit more, looking for some exposed flank to work on when something hard smacks me from behind, sending my head ringing. I don't pass out, but I'm staggering around, nauseous. Four ouncers have come out of the pub, big shiny dusters over their gloves, ready to give it to us. Batesy's booting one of the lads in the arse while Billy tries to prise his hands away from his face so he can do him some harm. He sees what's happened to me, stamps on the lad's knuckles then runs into the thick of the bouncers, jumping hard and butting the nearest one right under his nose. The shock of this assault by such a small lad wins it for us. They don't know what to do and just sort of crouch together and beckon us on to them with their hands, backing very slowly towards the pub as though there's wildcats in the yard and any sudden movement might prompt another savaging. There's silence except from the groans of the three Halifax pricks on the floor. One gets to his knees. Batesy boots him back down with a murderous kick in the gut. He must've ruptured something, there. The ouncers jump back towards us. Elvis flies in with his Stanley flashing. That's it. Given the perfect excuse to flee, three of them leg it back into the pub while the fourth, and slowest, gets cut across his arse. Elvis goes into the pub after him, slashing wildly and emerges seconds later, cackling:

'They've locked themselves in the shitter. Had the dance-floor to meself.'

We chuckle at this, doubting it, and start to vacate the scene. Elvis hoofs one of the crawling, coughing Halifax boys in the throat and we walk away, pleased with a job well done.

The square is chaos. Busies are swarming everywhere, nicking every likely head and lobbing them in the Maria. We turn and head back the way we've just come and turn right into the parallel street. It's a bit dicey. We have to pass a succession of moody-looking pubs and we're hardly inconspicuous with our hairstyles, bright jumbos, ski-jumpers and green Peter Storms. It must be too weird for these backward mobs getting ragged by us. We must look so . . . odd.

My arse goes a bit when we see a mob of Halifax up ahead, but as Elvis points out, they're probably shit scared of us. They'd run from the four of us if we gave it a little charge. He's great to be around at times like this, Elvis. His confidence is supreme. If I ever stopped to remember that his arrogance is based on the premise that you can't get hurt by a subby in wide trousers then maybe I'd leg it, too. But for now, with him, we're untouchable.

The route out of town to the ground gets very weird, taking us along tree-lined avenues and grand old houses similar to Oxton, but made of yellow-white York stone. I'm very relieved now that I didn't follow through the plan to jump Suzy. The crowd ahead veer down an acute left turn, and there's The Shay, Halifax's oval ground, below us. Outside a pub is the gladdening sight of Marty's red bonce and the rest of The Pack laughing and screwing up their faces and making punching gestures as they re-tell their stories. We get a little cheer from the lads as we amble down towards them, waving heroically.

'Fuckenell, boys, Hardy said youse'd got nicked!' shouts a much more cheerful Marty. Batesy makes him feel the lump on my head. Danny gets the ale in. The news from the hospital is not bad. Damien's wounds are superficial, due to him wearing a thick, £45 Marco Polo sweatshirt under his ski jumper. He's had a few stitches and has to rest. John is bad, but he'll live. Only now do I give full vent to the notion that he might have died back there.

The game's a cracker and everyone gets into it for a change. We must have 400 there including quilts and I'm sure that our loud, drunken vocal support helps Tranmere keep going in quagmire conditions to sneak a 2–1 win a few minutes from the end courtesy of a flying Mark Palios header. Halifax try to invade the pitch in a lame attempt at getting the game abandoned, but Marty and Batesy actually push our crew back, won't let us respond. The ref allows an eternity of injury time but the Rovers hang on and make it to the Third Round for the first time since 1971, when we got Stoke at home and 25,000 turned up.

The second biggest cheer of the day goes up at half time, when Damien materialises in our end, arm in a sling and grinning broadly. Marty gives him a little slap, but it's obvious he's made up to see his little brother's alright. Damien tells how he had to discharge himself when the duty doctor started insisting that he stayed in overnight. His voice squeaks with outrage as he points at his Adidas Barrington Gold:

'Stay in Halifax! Fuck that! Have all the sub-species crawling all over me gear in the middle of the night, trying to have it away!'

John Godden has told Damien we have to wait for him in The Rose and Crown. He's going to try and do one as soon as they take the drip off him. This suits us fine, as the draw for the next round is live on *Grandstand* at five past five, and Tranmere are in it! The Busies have other ideas. They want to keep us in while they try and disperse a revenge-crazed mob of Yorkie madmen, but we're more than keen to lend a hand. We heave at the old tongue and groove gates, feeling them buckle and splinter under our weight. I feel a bit sorry for the stooped old gate steward, who probably gives these gates a lick of blue paint every first of August and has never seen his ground treated with such brutish contempt. The gates suddenly just split and pop, a proper mini-explosion which must be the chains snapping, and we spill out all over each other into the street.

It's a bit of a game of tag between us, the plod and the Halifax revenge committee, with our crew rapidly replacing the local boys as the Busies' number one target. We give them the slip easily and start chasing ghosts. Halifax have talked themselves up over binfuls of ale, but they don't really want to know. There's one big mob of them standing off on a garage forecourt on the other side of the main road. Forgetting it's their yard and they're supposed to take the initiative, they start bellowing at us and pushing each other forward, starting a surge then stopping dead as imaginary policepersons, luckily for us, push them back. This maddens Billy, for some reason, who decides he's going to take the lot of them and goes haring across the road, screaming at them. To our great hilarity, they back off before a few big tough guys get round him and start wellying him. That's it. We're over the road and before we get within ten yards, Halifax are showing us their Wigan Casino patches. I can't be arsed going after them again. I want to hear the draw. So does Elvis. About thirty of us manage to detatch ourselves and get to The Rose and Crown, just after the draw has started.

'Who've Tranmere got, mate?' chirps Elvis at some gnarled curmudgeon.

'Hasn't come out yet,' he glowers back.

'I'll gi' you tuppence forrit,' says Elvis, nonesensically, trying to sound Yorkshire.

The draw drags on, then suddenly it's us, number twenty-seven, at home against . . . number three. Three eternities dawdle by. Liverpool. Fuck! Me and Elvis make open-mouthed faces at each other and start hugging Hardy, Danny, all the boys in the pub. Even Selwyn Froggit gets hugged, much to his disgruntlement.

'Buy this man a drink!' declares Elvis, stabbing his finger into one of the old man's hideous yellow warts. That just about does it for Old Silas. He drains his half of mild and sweeps up his tweed cap off the bar.

'I've had quite enough of your hospitality, thank you very much,' he says, old-geezering his way to the door, stopping, red-veined eyelids blinking back at Elvis and trying to sound cutting.

'I'll bid you goodnight.'

He touches his cap as he exits. This must be what is meant by 'bluff', when they talk of commonsense, down-to-earth, unattractive Yorkshire folk. The mob start filtering back into the pub. They tell of a convincing rout in a place called The People's Park but are cut short by our far sexier tales of Liverpool at home in the Cup. As more and more pack into the pub and the word goes round, Christmas suddenly arrives. There's a heady feel of celebration, everyone's getting the ale in, I even see the Thingwall boys pluck up the confidence to raise thumbs to Hardy and Baby. John Godden could not have picked a better moment to rejoin his estimable comrades.

He's cheered loudly, a chair is found for him in now claustrophobic conditions and no fewer than eight dozen menfolk seek his opinion on the Liverpool draw. It is, by common consent, sound. John is talking quietly to Marty about the stabbing incident, about which he remembers little, when Elvis pulls up a stool and starts pushing his ear closer and closer to Godden's lips. Godden stares down his nose at him.

'Wha'?'

'W-weird!!', shouts Elvis, making the double-u last forever.

'What?'

'No. Nothing.'

'Look, you funny cunt, what the fuck's up with you!?'

'Just, like, you sound okay. Early days, like, but I thought that with all that Yorkie blood they pumped into you you'd start talking ecky thump.'

There's a beat while this sinks in then the whole pub's in pleats, Godden himself laughing painfully.

'Do one, you, you weird bollix!'

The journey home is a merry one. By the time we draw in at Lime Street, we've hyped ourselves into a mob of fervent Scouse-haters and everyone's up for storming the Yankee Bar. We'll never have a better crew or a better opportunity so it's a deadly letdown when a hundred-odd of us walk into Liverpool's legendary stronghold to find it packed out with Christmas revellers and drunken old girls singing rebel songs. There's one or two heads in the back bit who cannot make out who the fuck we are. They know we're nothing to do with The Road End, and The Yankee is not somewhere you'd expect Everton to go socially. Eventually one of them comes over, horrible kite on him, nasty, narrow eyes and a bit of a scar on his temple. He starts trying to pal up to us, asking what the game was like. Marty pushes his way over.

'We're Tranmere. That's what you want to know isn't it, you Odgie cunt.'

'Tranmere.'

He just repeats the word, mulls it over quietly amused, then pulls a wincing face. He's cool. Not remotely flustered by the odds of a hundred and seventeen to five. Ugly, but cool. Batesy, with commendable valour and utter stupidity stands up.

'You've just met The Pack, lar!'

Suddenly it's my turn to wince. I glance at Elvis. All of a sudden our steely, streetwise little crew sounds like a bunch of drama students playing at being football thugs. Why do we have to have a name, anyway? The Scouse lad smiles to himself.

'Well. We'll be seeing youse then, The Pack.'

He walks back to his mates. Moments later a big laugh goes up. I flash a look at Marty. He shakes his head.

'Can't do five of 'em,' he moans.

'What if *five* of us do five of them?'

I'm up for it. That deformed little twat'll be a walkover. Marty won't have it.

'It's not on. It'll be playing into the cunts' hands.'

I don't see how but I say nothing.

The five Scousers drink up and leave, slowly, hands behind their backs, big sovereigns on their fingers, leather Wolfe jackets hanging off their shoulders and nice, strapover trainies. Not a Peter Storm among them – every one of our crew has bought one in the past week. Late again. They've got ironic, hunched-up walks and I notice each one slips a hand inside his pocket as they pass us. They nod their heads to the jukey and laugh as they go. Batesy's going mad. He runs after the last one, boots him up the arse and sticks his finger in his throat.

'Tell the pwicks on the Southside that we walked up and down Limey and no cunt wanted to know!'

The lad looks at Batesy for several seconds and then says:

'The pwicks on the Southside'll be sorry they missed you.'

That's it. Batesy butts him, there's a struggle in the doorway, Batesy throws more wild punches and finally loses a tug-of-war as he tries to haul the lad back into the bar as his mates pull him free from outside. For all that Batesy's some kind of whopper, he's ours and he's hard and he's the only of us who had a go. I'm glad he did what he did. I saw the look in the Scouser's eye. He was the real thing, for sure, but he wasn't used to people giving him a dig. He didn't like it. I wonder, in all seriousness, if we can get a result off this shower when they come to ours.

I touch lucky on two counts. I manage to geg in on a taxi to Parkgate with Sammy and Natasha, two girls in the year above Molly at Birkenhead High. She likes Natasha and we often see the two of them surrounded by the Cricket Club crew in The Old Quay, but it's Sammy who lets me suck her tits and finger her outside her house before pulling away, just like that, and bidding me a coy goodnight. I fall asleep downstairs in the middle of a wank over her.

10 December 1979

Over which Molly gives me hell. She found me there last night, sitting in the armchair, kecks around my ankles, knob aflop between my legs. She's been roasting me since I brought the drinks over.

'Impressive girth, though, bruv. Girth. Isn't that a smashing word. *Girth*. Mmm. Haven't come across a girth like that myself, yet. You've got quite a soss on you, haven't you?'

'I sincerely hope you haven't seen *any* girth, thank you very much.'

'Oh pur-lease! Spare me the protective older brother mularkey! Of course I've had cock! Lots of it!'

I look round, embarrassed. It's only just gone twelve, and The Old Quay is mercifully empty still. Molly smirks at me gleefully.

'Don't you want to know if I swallow? You want to know if your little sister gives good head, don't you?'

'We don't give head in Parkgate, Cheshire, honey. Don't say silly things.'

'What would you prefer me to call it, then?'

She affects a very unconvincing Nerys Hughes Liverpool accent.

'A better nosh?'

It dawns on me, belatedly, that she's raw with me about something.

'What's up, sis?'

She rolls her eyes at the ceiling.

'What's up, he asks, in all innocence.'

She looks away for inspiration and flashes back at me.

'I mean, how would *you* like it? How would you like it if you walked in one night and I'm sat there with my legs wide open and my mott hanging out?'

I consider this.

'I'd probably slide it right in there.'

She smacks me on the arm in a you're-not-taking-me-seriously sort of way and half-turns away on her stool, sulking. I crane my head and shoulders over the table so that I'm right in her face, gurning at her, trying to force a smile. I force a smile.

'C'mon, Moll. What's up?'

She sighs long.

'Everything. You.'

Now it's me hitting the significant sigh button.

'Look. I'm sorry you found me in a . . . compromised situation, but – you know, lads *do* that sort of thing. We wank. Constantly.'

She grimaces.

'You shouldn't. It's what everyone else does. It's cheap. You're not just one of the lads.'

'I am.'

'You're not!'

'Am too!'

'Not!'

'Am!'

'Am!'

'Not!'

She squeals with pleasure at catching me out, then fixes me with a disdainful little pout.

'What's the *matter* with you?'

I pretend to give this serious thought.

'I am the product of a blank generation. I live for kicks. I live for me.'

'You know that isn't true.'

She's getting me rattled, here. She leans over, irritatingly soft voice, now.

'So why say it? What's getting you, Paul?'

This is too much.

'What's getting *me*? I don't think I'm the one who should be under the microscope here! I *do* things! I go out. I'm interested in things. What's getting me! What's getting *you*! Or what are you not getting?'

I lean forward for the kill and jab a finger at her with the word 'that'.

'*That* is the question, is it not? Hmmm?'

I wave my chin up in the air, unsure of myself, unsure how Molly is going to react to this. I dearly wish I had not said it. I reckon without old brimstone herself.

'I'm not quite clear what I'm being accused of here, Paul. But if you're trying to suggest that my virginity is a situation that's being prolonged with any sense of reluctance on my part, then you're absolutely wrong.'

So calm. Why can't I be like that?

'I don't have a stance on sexual morality. For my own part, I haven't met a man – or a boy – who I like and fancy sufficiently to let him fuck me. And, again, for my own part – which is paramount in matters of sex and me – I don't yearn for cock so forlornly that I'm prepared to allow any of the inadequates I've met so far anywhere near my cunt. While I have a choice in the matter, I'm not going to engage in any activities which I might regret in later life. If I don't wholly believe that I'm special, what's the rest of the world to think? 'Nother drink?'

And she's off to the bar, all turbulent russet mane and sexual frustration. I watch her stride across the floor, a star in the making, and feel a knot in my stomach. I adore her. I wish that she weren't my sister.

Peter Elias, one of the big cheeses at work, comes in with a small, roly-poly, tight-curled woman. His wife, totally lacking any femininity. Why do women let that happen to them? Look at Molly, and look at her. And look at him. Peter Elias, feared by tax-dodgers all over Birkenhead 2 District. It's quite a shock, seeing him outside of the work environment. I recall seeing my Primary School teacher, Mrs Sidall, in the Co-Op in Neston, asking for fifteen milk tokens when I was about eight. It was an impossible thrill for me just to come across her like that, going about her normal life outside of her gubernatorial role. I just stood and stared at her, until she became aware of me and said hello, causing me to blush deeply and fall madly in love with her. I don't feel quite the same about Peter Elias, although it is strangely satisfying to think that we're all part of the same funny little pointless world.

Natasha comes in and makes a big thing of standing on her tiptoes and looking round the pub for someone. I wave her over, which she seems grateful for. She sits down and eyes me slyly.

'Sammy hasn't been in, has she?'

I make no bones about it.

'Probably wouldn't be sitting here with me!'

Natasha's all faux-intrigued.

'O-oh?'

I don't let her down.

'Afraid I behaved *disgracefully* last night. I don't expect she'll ever forgive me.'

I've never had Natasha all to myself before. She's stunning – a smaller, more mischievous, less ghostly Morticia off The Addams Family. Same blunt, Cleopatra fringe, long, black hair, moist red lips. But she's never been a sexual prospect, Natasha. It's always been widely-known that she's a great laugh and pretty wild, but don't expect any change. Knowing this does nothing to prevent my melodramatic attempt at a screen kiss. Natasha laughs and gives me a friendly push.

'You beast! What did you *do* to my friend!'

I see Molly returning with the drinks. I wink at Natasha.

'Gents don't spill.'

'Shouldn't stop you then, Paul Carty!'

'I like to maintain a certain level of discretion. As you'll appreciate when we acquiesce to our destiny . . . to be lovers!'

She gasps and makes a wide-eyed, shocked-at-the-cheek-of-it face, but is prevented from answering by Molly plonking the drinks down. She barely acknowledges her friend.

'Paul, why are you putting on that ridiculous accent. He's got 9 O-levels, you know, Tash, and he tries to sound like he's from the Woodchurch!'

She's almost right. I suppose I do lay the accent on thick, sometimes, especially when I'm with The Pack, but I modulate it for all sorts of situations. I can go very posh indeed when I'm in Gilmartin's. I try to give people what they want – or what they expect, at least. I'm only doing it with Natasha because all the posh girls love a bit of rough. For a surgeon's daughter, she puts on a bit of a dialect herself. She gives me a protective hug.

'Oh, but he's *sweet*, though!'

'You wouldn't say that if you'd met his friends and saw what they get up to.'

I didn't know that Molly had any inkling about my extra-curricular activities. I certainly don't want it broadcast in front of Peter Elias, a man who is only aware of me as a keen young man he sees leaving the office late and who comes highly commended by Bob McNally. There's only one way to get her off her hobby-horse. I'm very reluctant to do this, but . . .

'Moll's having one of her let's-play-Mum days. She only has them once or twice a year.'

Molly's eyes are burning into me. Mine blaze back at her with equal fury.

'But she shouldn't torment herself. She knows she can never be Mum.'

Moll just sits there, looking at me, expressionless. Her eyes fill up. I feel like shit. Natasha gets up, embarrassed, and clears her throat.

'If you *do* see Sammy, tell her I've gone The Red Lion.'

I don't know why, but I have to hurt Molly some more.

'*To* The Red Lion, Tash. You're in company, don't forget.'

Molly gets up and manages to steer her svelte carriage to the Ladies with grace. Natasha shoots me a look and goes after her. I look out over the marsh, feeling low. How could I do it to her? I knew it'd destroy her. I really don't like me, at times. There was no need for that. I could've soaked it up and turned it into a joke, but I had to defend myself, had to fight back. What a dismal little cunt. Natasha returns and makes it clear that she's not staying.

'What'd she say?'

'Oh – just that you're all she's got left and she can see you're slipping away. You know – girlie stuff.'

I blush again. Natasha gives me a peck on the cheek and leaves. Molly comes back to the table. She dabs her eye and smiles weakly.

'I'm sorry,' she says.

I shake my head and take her hand and feel my throat tightening. I can't say anything so I sit and look at her and swallow hard on my tears. Molly kisses a fingertip and holds it to my lip and lowers her head to catch my eyeline. Her smile is happier now.

'I just love you so much,' she says. 'Please don't shut me out. I need you. For the time being.'

I smile and wipe my eyes with the back of my sleeve. She offers me a tissue. I shake my head and take a long swig of my pint. I breathe in deeply and feel better.

'I dunno, Moll. I've got to sort things out.'

'Yes. Me too.'

'Friends again?'

'Always.'

Strolling back home, arm in arm like a couple of lovers, we

make fun of everything. In the Cricket Club car park, a purple-faced zealot is making the most of what's left of the light by washing his Daimler, patiently carrying bowls of water out from the clubhouse and hurling them over his car.

'D'you imagine he's trying to wake it up?' giggles Molly.

This has us chuckling all the way home and it doesn't seem to matter much when we get in and Dad tells us that one of his old suppliers is buying the house. We have to be out by the end of March.

11 December 1979

Elvis is being somewhat weird. He calls me at work to say he doesn't fancy the game tonight, but he wouldn't mind going out somewhere later – maybe even The Chelsea. Tranmere versus Rochdale on a bitter Monday night not so long before Christmas with very little at stake is a resistable proposition, in the normal scheme of things. Except that this is what we do. We go to Tranmere. We've been going to Tranmere, individually and now together, for years.

I've been attending extravaganzas of soccer wizardry at Prenton for a decade. My first game was against Bury in February 1969, one of only three occasions when a near neighbour, Mr Coleman, took me, and I've been going ever since. I've seen us play Bradford Park Avenue and Barrow, both long since gone, though not Accrington Stanley. It would never occur to me to miss a game. While everyone else in my class was reaping the rewards of following Liverpool and Everton, with a few miscreants deciding they liked Leeds after they won the League, I was loyally making my way, alone, to Prenton Park to support Tranmere Rovers.

There was a magic about Friday-night football, floodlit and only semi-real as heroic figures like George Yardley and Kenny Beamish scored audacious-seeming goals within touching distance. My rare trips to Anfield with schoolmates seemed antiseptic by comparison.

It was a solitary experience. I began to stand in the same place every game, on the Borough Road side of the Cowshed, but without the back-up of any gang or mates, I never risked letting on to any of the lads I started to recognise as regulars. I didn't mind. I liked doing it this way. It was a part of me that was mine.

One of the faces I'd always see, way back, was Elvis. Always with a little mob of urchins, Elvis would spend most games roaming the ground, climbing the floodlight stanchions, sneaking into the back of the wooden snack bar on the Open End, baiting the police and the away fans. Him and his little crew were a regular sideshow.

This one time, about 1974, Blackburn brought a good mob of beefy Soul Boys, about 150 of them, all dressed in white parallels, Martens and elasticated cord bombers. I thought they looked sound. Elvis was with the Mini WEBB in the Cowshed. At that time there was a lot of inter-estate skirmishing, with the big mobs like the NEBB (North End Boot Boys) and the BABB (Bomb Alley Boot Boys) launching spectacular raids on each others' territory but the Woody boys were fine with Elvis. Each gang had a junior faction, of which the mini-Woodchurch were the most numerous and famously naughty. The Mini-WEBB always came to Tranmere. Where the young Ford kids might drift across to Liverpool, or Leasowe and Moreton were Everton strongholds, there was almost a religion, a received wisdom on the Woodchurch that they were the defenders of the faith. Woodchurch, Rock Ferry, Downtown and the North End formed Tranmere's hardcore, but sometimes even they didn't bother turning up.

The Blackburn, finding no opposition in the Open End, walked right around the side of the Borough Road and came onto the corner of the Cowshed to find themselves confronted by a snarling pack of twelve- and thirteen-year-olds, chanting at them in high-pitched voices. The Blackburn stopped and guffawed, feigning to run and, when the Mini-WEBB tore after them, stopped and turned, laughing. There was a standoff of a few seconds, all the little Woody skins bouncing, ready to go.

'Back to school on Monday!' sang the Blackburn mob, still

amused by this plucky little firm. I think I was excited, genuinely thrilled by football violence for the first time when all the Woodchurch rats, Elvis in the thick of them, ran into the Blackburn blokes and starting peppering them, swarming all over them, digging them and butting them. For a second Blackburn backed off down the terracing, unsure whether it was okay to hit back at a bunch of kids. Elvis' crew carried on, really giving it to them, picking up the lumps of concrete and broken masonry that littered the back of the Cowshed, savaging the Blackburn contingent. I was gripped. This was a real underdog scrap, much more exciting than the stolid game of checkmate on the pitch, and Tranmere were getting the upper hand. Not for long. Blackburn regrouped and stormed into the Woody, scattering them. Elvis and a few others ran back into them again, but by now the four police on duty had ambled around to the fracas and started herding a compliant Blackburn firm back towards the Open End.

'Shit ow-ziz, nah-nah-nah, shit ow-ziz, nah-nah-nah,' sang the Mini WEBB, to the tune of 'Banana Splits'. Blackburn didn't sing back. Way after midnight that night I was still turning over the events in my mind. It was the closest I'd ever come to a real rumpus and by far the most exciting thing I'd ever seen at first hand.

I'd watched some of Elvis' finest moments over the past few years, while making my fortnightly supplication to TRFC. All I'd ever wanted was to get to know the crew, go to the aways with them, support the Rovers properly. Now that it's mine I'm not so sure, but I never reckoned with Elvis getting tired of it all. I suppose I always thought that I'd give it up first.

I go to the game, stand with Batesy. Apart from him and Billy and a couple of the others, the lads're a bit funny with me. A couple of ciggy butts hit me on the back of the head during the first half and someone keeps playing that tiresome game where you tap someone on the shoulder, or flick them on the ear, and everyone's staring straight ahead when you turn round. So I don't turn round. I watch the match more studiously than usual. It's shite. Tranmere lose 2–1 in spite of playing the majority of the second half in Rochdale's goalmouth, but breakaway goals either side of half time steal if for the visitors, who are applauded wildly at the final whistle by the twenty-five quilts who've made the journey. There's halfhearted talk of leathering them, a move so unethical that it's almost worth doing – not that my opinion is being counselled on the matter. Is this all because Elvis isn't here to validate me? I fucking hope not, the shower of no-marks. I'm tickled nonetheless at the thought of pure hammering a load of kagoul-clad surveyors, but no one can be arsed. The mob, as well as the team, are suffering a bit of a hangover from the F.A. Cup.

I decide to walk back into town, where I'm meeting Elvis in The Letters. It's only a fifteen-minute walk, and gives me time to brood. Does my standing in The Pack really depend upon the patronage of fucking Elvis? I unearth a bit of jealousy, a resentment that Elvis is actually taking steps to get out of his situation while I'm still here, still wanting to kick fuck out of some poor cunt from Rochdale, all in the name of Tranmere Rovers whose elected representatives can just as happily do without my services. And what *about* this violence, anyway. What's all that about? Dunno. Not appalled by it like most people. Whole people. I'm just . . . used to it. I'm not a bastard but . . . I just don't see what the big deal is. The world is violent.

Elvis, thankfully, is not smug and superior as only he can be when he's discovered an unheard-of band or a new brand of trainies (Donnay is his latest 'find'). I'd braced myself for a condescending, almost pitying enquiry about the match followed by some grand revelation – he's off to Prague in January to live with some disenfranchised countess he met at a Psychedelic Furs gig in London, or he's off to work on a kibbutz. But no. He's quiet, listless, very, very down.

Two pints and two large vodkas do nothing to lift our spirits. Elvis only becomes more edgy, complaining when I don't drink as fast as him. Then he says it.

'Dja reckon you can see us right for a bit of a dropsy? Just till after Chrimbo, like?'

I must look very shocked indeed. Elvis *always* has money. Lots of money. Always.

'Salright. Forget it.'

'How much, like?'

'Nah. Forget it.'

'No, come 'ead. You've bailed me out enough times.'

Pathetically, I pull out a couple of fivers and six or seven smooth new pound notes, which I got out of the autobank in Hamilton Street only an hour before, neatly packaged in a perspex clip. He looks at the money a little too long, as though he's considering dragging it out of my hands and eating it.

'No, honest, Cart. I'm thinking about getting off, like. Proper, like. I'd need poke for the move, but I need to think it all out, yet. Me swede's twatted. I don't know what to do.'

For a moment I feel like I should take his hand, but I can't think of any one person I'd feel less comfortable embracing – apart from my father. Elvis suggests we jib the club and go back to his for knives. He obviously wants to talk. I sense that I haven't heard the last of this loan proposition. We huddle round the small stove in his kitchen while the wide flat blades of the butter-knives blacken in the jet of the gas flame. A few nights ago I walloped the lovely Sonia in here. Elvis and her should get together and drag each other down. The fights'd be terrific. And I could step in and shag her behind his back. That'd show him who's boss.

He fits the jar over the heated knives and manipulates the pot to a smoking putty as I inhale greedily, keeping the smoke down until a woozy wave of nausea forces it back up and out again. I gasp, tears stinging my eyes, and try to hold onto my balance. I hear Elvis cackling.

'Steady on old fruit. That stuff's opiated. Take it easy. I need you to operate for me, yet.'

I work the blades together, squashing the hot hashish and sending a plume of thick smoke billowing into the jar. Elvis sucks it up smoothly, holds it in, smiles through his small, even, yellowish teeth and exhales. A hot-knives masterclass, perfectly executed.

He puts on a Love album. I know 'Alone Again Or' and a few others, but Arthur Lee doesn't really interest me. I'm not that arsed about old stuff. Even punk, revolutionary a couple of years ago, seems cartoonish now. I know Elvis is putting this on to place me into the role of the student – a relationship in which he's always revelled.

He pulls out a little brass pipe, pops a crumb of hash in and lights up, sucking madly on the pipe, flipping his thumb sporadically over the end of the funnel. He sucks for no more than thirty seconds then solemnly tips the pipe over, flicking at the funnel to empty any residue before breaking off another crumb of pot and passing the pipe over to me. I suddenly feel a powerful dread sensation, a closing in, a disorientating onset of panic and fear. I've got to get out of here.

I hold up the flat of my palm to indicate to Elvis that I don't want any more. He smirks slyly, as though this is some sort of victory. He leans back against a large beanbag, sparking up the pipe and sucking spasmodically until there's no more smoke. He holds his breath for ages and spews it out, laughing nastily. I'm legging it as soon as he goes to the bog. He carries on staring at me and laughing noiselessly, wheezily, those square yellow teeth taking the piss out of me.

'You think you're really . . . out there, don't you?' he says slowly, carefully.

My heart sinks. People say 'my heart sank' all the time, but my heart plummets several thousand feet at these, Elvis' first cruel words to me. Now I see it all. Him showing me. Showing me Tranmere, The Pack; taking me to The Cazza,

Peter Kavanagh's, The Crack, Michel Claire, The Swinging Apple, Neil's Corner, Sexy Rexy, The Chelsea; getting me affiliated. Elvis giving me my culture, my character, my life. And now he was going to snatch it all back again. He was giggling.

'You are though . . . you are,' he gasps, struggling to hold back the convulsions, the waves of laughter, striving to cap them.

'You're the . . . hahaha . . . you're . . . IT! You're close to the edge, man . . . hahahha! You're the real thing!'

I want to get up and leave but I'm rooted. Elvis leans over behind his speaker and pulls out a carved wooden box. Shit, standard, hippy stash-box. He pulls out a wrap, opens it out then jumps athletically to his feet in one bound. He returns from the kitchen with a cardboard bog-roll holder and a piece of foil. He also has his Stanley. But no fear. My panicky disorientation is over. If Elvis wants to know . . . I'm here. I've never thought about this before, but I can slam the little cunt if needs be. I know I can.

Elvis cuts the toilet roll in half with the Stanley. He stretches the foil over one end of the tube. He punctures half a dozen holes into the foil and sprinkles some coarse, sandy powder into the parabola. He ignites the powder and lies back, putting the other end of the cardboard tube into his mouth and sucking gently, slowly, keeping the flame burning over the powder at the other end. A few moments later he drops his zippo and flops out, breathing deeply and languorously, inhaling the last of the ashes and smiling over at me. The unhinged giggling monkey of a minute ago has gone. Elvis lies there, eyes pinned, just smiling at me. I get up.

'Gotta go,' I say, going.

I'm just pulling the living-room door behind me when I hear a hoarse but distinctive whisper.

'You're it, Carty, lar.'

Then I hear him crying.

15 December 1979

I've started seeing Sammy. Not that there's any great point to it besides the mouth exercise. I don't just mean her constant yacking, either – she's quite happy to lie upstairs on her little pink bed, legs asplay, teddies watching, while I munch her for hours on end. She gasps and gurgles like a delighted baby, but if I so much as edge the tip of my penis towards that unctuous slit, down comes the portcullis. Quite where the ethical divide lies, I don't know. Tongue-plating, good. Dobber, bad.

I'm seeing her for something to do, something regular that normal people do, just while I rationalise my life. I'm sitting with her, or, more properly, sitting opposite her in The Old Quay, when Molly walks in, looking frightful. She's walking round the pub, eyes wide and terrified, searching for something. My first thought is that she's dropped a trip, or someone's spiked her.

She eventually focuses upon me only when I'm halfway across the pub floor and almost on top of her. She talks in a slightly slurred, spaced-out voice.

'Oh. Paul. They said they'd seen you in here.'

'Who did? What's up, Moll?'

'The boys.'

It's only now that I properly take in the ripped strap on her favourite black 'stunner' dress, the tear just below the arm and the scratches on her shoulder and neck. My heart starts thumping painfully.

'Moll! What boys?'

She slumps down into the free chair and just stares at

Sammy and me, looking right through us with shocked, uncomprehending eyes.

'The . . . they. . . .'

It's like she's sleepwalking. She starts becoming troubled at her inability to tell me what's wrong. Sammy's surprisingly cool.

'I think you should call the police, Paul. And an ambulance. I'll stay with her.'

I jump up, wired but feeling useless, clueless. Sammy puts her arm around Molly. She's twigged way before I even allow myself to contemplate the possibilities. The word 'rape' is denied access.

'Paul. Ask if a WPC can attend, too.'

I nod, blankly. By the time I return from the phone, Sammy has ascertained that at least one youth, possibly more, has assaulted Molly outside a party at the Cricket Club. She hasn't been violated, but she's been badly knocked about. I remember now that Molly was going to this do and had asked me to come along. I despise the sort of big-boned Prince Andrew types who frequent the Cricket Club and I'd politely passed up the offer.

'It'll end in tears,' I'd said.

I'm tightening up inside. I know that I have to wait here with Molly, but how I want to get up there, find the twats and bite their faces off. Molly's shivering badly, not quite convulsing but definitely going that way. Simultaneously, Sammy and I fish our jackets off the back of our seats and cover her. Her teeth are chattering and she's emitting a barely-audible, one-pitch wail, like a lobster being boiled. I'm helpless. I want to hold her. I want to get up to the Cricket Club.

The ambulance arrives before the police, making my decision for me. I ask Sammy to ride with her. With it being Christmas the plod could be up to their eyebrows with seasonal bloodshed. They might be hours yet. I tell Sammy that I feel I should get along to the party, find out what exactly happened, get hold of witnesses and so on. She's fine about it. I tell her I'll phone Dad and we'll follow on as soon as possible.

I have never felt this way before. I am ice. I walk briskly the few hundred yards from The Old Quay to the party. I can hear the bass line thumping out from the clubhouse immediately I step outside. I'm not angry. I'm not scared. I have no emotional imbalance one way or the other. I'm going to do a job. And I won't be going anywhere else or thinking about any other thing until this is done. I turn into the driveway and stride towards the clubhouse. There are quite a few people outside. Raised voices. A female voice and a drunk, braying male. Closer, now, I see four lads, maybe another, too, sitting on a wall, watching the row, laughing and whistling. I recognise the girl at about the same time she sees me. She runs towards me and throws herself upon me, sobbing.

'Thank God! Oh, thank God! Did she find you?'

It's Emily, a classmate of Molly's from Heswall who's been round to ours a couple of times over the years. She's grown tall. Fucking hell. She's lovely.

'Woah! Slow down, Emily! What's going on here?'

Before she can answer me this square-chinned preppie gobshite comes walking over, smiling. *Smiling.* I'd want to club his teeth out with a mallet in any event, but he's walking up to me, smiling, confident and he thinks, this piece of shit thinks that he's going to say something to me.

'Saved by the cavalry, eh?'

He doesn't know how close he is to getting killed, here and now, right in front of his rugger-bugger prick mates. But I keep my fist in my pocket and decide to find out a few things.

'Who the *fuck* are you?'

My voice is blood on the rocks. He glances round at his friends, nervous for the first time. I know absolutely that this is my man. But still I need to know what he did to my sister. He tilts his chin at me and gives a sort of half-shudder. His upper lip is actually stiff. He has hateful curls. He looks at me sideways on, as if he's about to give the gardener a dressing-down. He has the most punchable general appearance that I have ever encountered. And in two or three minutes I am going to give him a hiding more savage than anything he's ever dreamed possible and then I'm going to drag him home by his curls and make him tell his parents what he's done.

'D'you know who you're talking to?' he says, sticking his chin out a little bit more. I can't help looking at my feet and smiling at this.

'Why don't you tell me? And you can tell me what the fuck you did to my sister while you're at it. I'm going to kill you anyway, but you may as well tell me what you did to her so's I don't have to kick it out of you.'

His arse goes, visibly, when I tell him he's just attacked my sister. He's shitting himself. But he's too thick and too pissed and just too much of a blood to back down. Emily speaks.

'This is Will Harnault, Paul.' She pronounces it Harno. 'Him and his chums decided they were entitled to rough me and Molly up a bit when we passed on their offer to go for a ride with them in their daddy's BMW. . . .'

'That's *very* dangerous talk, Emily. Do you know that I can sue you for talk like that?'

'Shut up, prick!'

He comes right up to me, quivering with affront. His mates jump down from the wall to get closer to the action. They're carrying sticks. Good. Let them come. As they pass under a street-light I see that three of them have cricket stumps. Not so good.

'Now listen, you! If your . . . *sister* thinks it's amusing to let chaps buy her drinks all night then suddenly start taking the piss out of them, she's got to be ready to take the consequences in good part.'

I smash him in the mouth. He's down on his knees, holding his face, coughing.

'What did you do to her, you' – I run over and grab his hair and yank his head back and growl the words at him through my jugulars, my teeth touching his nose. Before he can say anything one of the other goons comes running at me with a stump. He lashes at me wildly, missing my head by a clear yard without me having to duck. I kick him hard in the arse as he goes past me. Harno gets to his feet and stumbles back towards the clubhouse. I go after him. I hear Emily scream then, whack! Dark. That's it.

When I come to, there are three police vehicles in the car park, Emily is talking to Dad and one of the plod, and the music has stopped. Dozens of people are streaming past me. I've got a blanket over me and my head hurts more than anything I've ever known. An ambulance turns in to the driveway. I feel myself slipping away again.

16 December 1979

I'd been determined to see it through with Elvis, but I can't do this without him. I'm back where I started, completely within his gift, awaiting the nod of approval. It feels like starting over. My hand shakes as I dial, and I'm about to slam the phone down after only five or six rings.

'Hello?' He never gives the number. Just hello. I'm not prepared for the huge relief I feel when we talk. He's made up to hear from me. Genuinely. Neither of us makes reference to the night of the hot knives. Elvis says he'll get to work on sorting a little mob out. Get round here, pronto. I leave the house, immediately, not questioning, dancing once again to Elvis' tune. It doesn't matter that I'm rushing round to his. What matters is that he's helping me deal with Will Harnault. Only too pleased to.

Since we picked Molly up this morning I've been doing my research, finding out who they are and where they drink. Natasha, whose dad actually plays for Neston Cricket Club, came round to see Molly and brought his photo album with her. I wish I was going out with her. I don't even think I'd be that arsed about the sex – a chick like her would get into it in her own time. She's just so funny, and . . . *nice*. Molly's immediately looking better, sitting propped up in bed like Queen Victoria and laughing at Natasha's gags. She chides me for ignoring the pleas of the ambulance crew last night and staggering back home.

'Didn't want to give Dad any *more* shocks.'

'That's remarkably selfless of you.'

I'm falling in love with her, the raven-haired loony. I

powerfully want to lean over and hug her – as I'm sure she knows. She goes through her dad's photos with me and Moll. They're all in there. They come in The Old Quay occasionally, but they're more for The Red Lion and The Parkgate. I assure the girls that I'll go directly to the police with this information. They know that I won't.

I'm disappointed by how few of the lads turn up. Elvis has been on the phone all afternoon rallying the troops with lurid tales of gang rape in Parkgate and his feeling is that loads of heads'll turn out for me. We wait at The Cuckoo in Woodside, but only Batesy, Billy Powell and an astonishingly drunk Damien O'Connor show up. Batesy tries to soften the blow by explaining that John Godden's got a big thing on tonight which needed lots of backup. The only reason Batesy's here himself is that he's friendly with both factions in Godden's dispute. For all Batesy's good intentions, he only makes me feel bad that I wasn't considered worthy of John's fracas – whatever it may be. I thought he was starting to come round to me.

Just as we're crossing over to wait for the Neston bus, Danny Allen comes running up, out of breath. I'm immensely touched. Somehow, this makes a difference. Not just that Danny's a weather-vane, always keeping in with the majority, and he's chosen to go with me, but he's such an unapologetic shithouse, as well. He must realise that he's actually going to have to fight tonight. It's six onto, what – ten, fifteen? Doesn't matter. I feel as though with six of us we can make a bit of a noise. This is good, now.

The ride down to Parkgate is slow and uneventful, apart from Damien trying to force his head out of a tiny top deck window to be sick and finding himself stuck fast, with torrents of vom blowing back in his face. The smell of him is nearly enough to get us all going.

The bus stops just before The Parkgate Hotel. We hop off and, although everyone's jaunty, I'm feeling the tension more than ever. *I've* called this extraordinary general meeting, it's my problem and it's up to me to ensure that all goes well. I'm still concerned that I'm asking too much of them. I'm sure Elvis would've said if I was out of line in asking them to help with this, but the lack of support and the absurd sight of The Pack traipsing past the manicured lawns and ornamental ponds of The Parkgate Hotel is giving me serious pause for thought. Not even Elvis knows I live down here.

One glimpse of the back of Will Harnault's odious swede lays all my fears to rest. When they see these gobshites, these hooray Henrys and Harrys and Harnos who tried to rape my sister, the boys will thank me for dragging them all the way out here to assist with necessary redress. Damien staggers into the main bar, gloriously pickled, agape at all the posh fanny.

'Sound in here, isn't it? Can we stay and talk to the birds after the knuckle?'

I manage to persuade him back to a corner table, away from the hooting throng, while I point out the objects of our affection.

'They're all there, together, the ones who got me and the cunt who tried to rape Molly. There's a few more standing with them. I don't know if they're part of the clan or not but it's not going to matter. We'll just hit them with everything. They won't know what's going on. They'll shit, I tell you – they'll fuck each other right off and try and jump through those fucken windows.'

'D'you want me to cover the door and bang any cunt who twies to get out?' offers Batesy.

'I reckon you'll have more fun down there with me,' I say, getting up.

'Hang on!' slurs Damien. 'Aren't we at least having one bevvy before we go and fuck the place up?'

I'm just keen to get on with it. Billy shrugs his indifference but the others all take the view that, having come all this way, they wouldn't mind a drink before we get lobbed straight back out of this over-plush, over-pink hostelry. Elvis and I go to the little side bar. Down below I can clearly see the twat that whacked me last night and, leaning with his back to me, elbows on the bar, is Harnault. I catch the other lad's eye and wink at him. He goes white.

It's good to know that, while we're sipping lager-tops five yards away, the word is pinballing round the lounge that we're here and that there's going to be a ballroom blitz. You can smell the shite.

'What's this thing of John's, then?' I ask Batesy. He looks uncomfortable and tries to dismiss it.

'Just a bit of a score to be settled, like. You'll hear about it.'

Billy offers a barely discernible shake of his head. Batesy wanders over to the door and kicks it shut, glancing down into the main area on his way back.

'Still there?' I ask. He nods.

'Few of them. All huddled together, talking themselves up. I say we just go over now and slam them. Fucken mash the cunts. They won't know what's hit 'em'.

Billy nods.

'Might've called the Busies, anyway. Never know with these well-to-do fellas, do you?'

'They're the worst ones,' I say. 'Come 'ead. Let's do it.'

We get up, leaving fullish pints, and amble down the three steps leading into the busy main bar area. I'm not certain, yet, how I'm going to kick this off – all I do know is that it's my call and I have to do it right. Harnault's crew – miraculously there's about ten or twelve of them now – are waiting, tense, and step back a few paces as we come down the steps. You can see their utter bemusement at the sight of little Billy and Damien, who both look like our kid brothers. I did all the talking I needed to do last night and see little point in prolonging the foreplay. I spring down the last step and throw myself at Will Harnault, butting him full in the face and following with a flurry of shots to the side and back of his head as he tries to rugby-tackle me round the waist and heave me over. None of his mates get involved. A space clears as they surround us and for a moment it's schoolboy wrestling. I can feel my strength starting to sap. I don't go in for this endurance type of combat. He's fucking strong, Harnault, and I know that if I don't get some good digs in now, he's going to overpower me. I prise my arms free and this time get one, two, three cracks into his face. He slips, grabs at me to steady himself and punches fresh air. He's bleeding from his mouth, his nose and a bad cut above his cheekbone, where I butted him. He's wobbling badly, now, breathing heavy and trying to laugh as though there's nothing for him to worry about and his best is yet to come. I make for him, stand off a second, crouch to get a proper look, then smash him in the balls with my left foot. As he doubles, winded, I put the boot in his face and, not convinced that I've connected cleanly, I pull his head back and kick him again, satisfied that this time I've felt something – his teeth or maybe his jaw – crack. He goes limp and I let him slide down my shins, groaning.

This, it seems, is just not cricket. Bristling with outrage and determined to teach us some manners, Will's chaps start pushing our lot, poking them in the chest or shoving them with the flats of their hands in such a way as to let it be known that they wish the opposition to strike the first blow. A foolhardy strategy. A squat, powerful-looking sporty ted, spotless face, flawless teeth, Enid Blyton looks, gets on his tiptoes and sticks his forehead in Batesy's face, not butting him, but stag-like, trying to push Batesy back with his nut. Batesy's face twists up, making him look 124. He sways to one side. The rugger-ted tries to sway with him, keeping his head glued to Batesy's. Batesy has a swift and devastating solution to this. He punches both sides of the lad's head with both of his gigantic, ugly fists. It's like Tom and Jerry, where Tom gets his head slammed inside two cymbals and stands there, vibrating madly on the spot. Batesy, unnecessarily maybe, swipes up a glass and gives it him in the chops. He screams like a pig, turning round and round in blind circles, bits of glass sticking out of the side of his face and blood running in criss-cross squiggles down his cheeks. This is not a young man who set out tonight, or ever, dreaming that he might get glassed. The place goes deathly. Will's crowd are sickened, rooted to the spot, gaping. Nobody goes to help the lad, whose squealing is plain embarrassing now. Then they start running, all of them, running, pushing each other over, trampling on each other to get away from us.

Danny and Damien are chasing two knobs round the bar. Danny, who I've never seen fighting before, is booting some cunt up the arse and digging him right round his shoulder, getting him in the face from behind. Old Bill any second, I'm sure. Billy Powell has got some lad over a table, banging his head against its edge. Two of his mates run over.

'Enough!' they yell. One of them tries to pull Billy off from behind but succeeds only in getting a wild elbow jabbed in his eye.

'Like fuck!' screams Billy, spinning round and facing these two. 'Was it enough last night when you was getting into them girls?'

The two lads are ashen. The one whose head Billy has been pounding against the table looks up, groggily. Billy rams his head back into the wrought-iron table rim. You can hear the crack from where I am. I hope it's just his nose.

'Enough, you fucking savage!' shrieks one of them, looking properly sickened by what he's seen. Elvis strolls across to him.

It's starting to get me now that I live round here and it's not going to trouble the plod too much to route this carnage back to me. It's one thing avenging an attempted rape on your sister, on the spot, on the night, but they could really trump this one up. Elvis pulls out his Stanley and slices the lad from his forehead to his chin with one horrible, scimitar-shaped stripe.

'Enough,' says Elvis. He walks casually to the door, stopping to wipe his blade on the curtains. The rest of them follow him. I'm still in shock and starting to tremble a bit, post ag. I go over to Will, who's now, shakily, back on his feet. I loathe him more passionately than ever and for a second it feels like I'm going to do him again. But I don't. I take his square face in between my finger and thumb and squeeze hard. I hear sirens outside. More than one car.

'Don't say one fucken word!' I hiss. I try to pinch his face as hard as I can, but he starts whimpering and grabbing my sleeve and trying to apologise. I'm sure that if I threaten the whole pub to say fuck all to the Busies, they're scared enough to comply. Even the onlookers. But I know my voice won't hold out. I'm choked. There's bleeding, moaning, broken dick-heads everywhere. I'm choked but I'm fucking proud of the way we went about this. No messing. I want to do a look that tells The Parkgate Hotel that I'll come back for anyone who speaks to the coppers, but instead I find myself hurrying out, fighting back nausea. I get out and over one of the dinky little timber bridges before chucking up pure bile into the pond.

The boys are nowhere to be seen. Not surprising, with squad cars racing up the hotel's asphalt drive and Busies crawling everywhere but the place where the trouble was. I stick to the trees and hop over a mesh fence into someone's garden, then out and away past The Boathouse and onto the marsh. It's dry enough if you stick close to the harbour wall, even this time of year, and you're well out of sight from the road.

I half-crawl along the front past The Ship before I feel safe in re-emerging up the stone steps onto the prom. I'm about to make a dash down the side entrance to Mostyn House and get back home that way, when something catches my eye. Someone's sitting there in the eerie, apocalyptic half-light, just sitting there on the bench, staring out at the damp, and the blinking lights of Flint and Mostyn. It's Elvis. It's Elvis and he's crying, snuffling fitfully and sucking his breath in in fits and starts. I don't think he's seen me.

'El!' I hiss. He turns round, sharply.

'Who's that?'

'Carty!' Beat. 'Paul!'

He gets up, slowly, walks to me, slowly, and throws his arms around me, hugging me tightly and snivelling on my shoulder. I'm not alarmed by this, so much, but I've certainly never known him to be agitated, emotional like this. He's unrecognisable, tears streaking his face.

'Paul!' Beat. 'Mate!'

I don't know what to say. I sort of put my arms around him, weakly, and instantly remove them. He hardly ever calls me Paul.

'I'm so sorry,' says Elvis.

'Why?' I say, trying to feel out the eye of his distress. 'I asked you to come. You did me proud.'

Elvis shakes his head, vehemently. He looks out over the marshy Dee and, eventually, speaks again. He's much calmer. He looks right at me.

'I did me proud. I done it for me. So's it'd all finish up okay. Me 'n' you, like. I couldna left it like that.'

I nod, unsure. I see now that he's stroking the blade of his Stanley between thumb and finger, cutting himself.

'That's it now. That's the last time.'

He hurls his blade into the marsh and turns to face me.

I hold his look. I put one hand on his shoulder.

'You did it for me,' I insist. 'I'll never forget it.'

He cracks the slightest of smiles, looks down again, shaking his head, and this time comes back up laughing, still shaking his head. He's mad, Elvis. He's always been mad. One of my defining memories of him was this one time we were playing Barrow. I was twelve. Barrow only brought about forty, but a few grock-types were sitting on a barrier in the Open End, letting it be known that they didn't give a fuck. Elvis, who just looked like a kid, walked across the Open End in a pair of Jesus sandals, stood in front of the Barrow ogres and challenged them to stamp on his toes. They wouldn't, obviously. 'Shitbags!' sqeaked little El and sauntered back into the Borough Road shed. I remember trying to grin my approval, but he blanked me.

'Come 'ead,' I say, patting him on the back. 'Time for you to stay at Carty Acres.'

There seems no point in my being embarrassed about our palatial homestead any more. It won't matter what anyone thinks now. Somehow I know that this is the end. I'm fine about it. Tranmere, Elvis, whatever – I think this is as far as we go.

We jog across the road and up the Mostyn House drive. I turn to show Elvis the easiest part of the playing-field wall to get over, but he's gone. I laugh to myself; then louder.

'NICE ONE, ELVIS!' I shout.

17 December 1979

It's just gone eleven when they call. Although I'm more than half-expecting it, my heart jerks when the doorbell goes and sinks when I peer through the little blown-glass spy window to see two burly coppers. I'm just glad that Molly and Dad've gone for a constitutional on the Wirral Way.

I invite them inside. I feel and, I know, look guilty as fuck. I have to get out of the room and compose myself and start again. I was just making tea when they called and I ask them if Darjeeling's alright. I suppose I'm trying to show them that I'm class – not at all the sort who'd maim a nice, curly-headed lad out with his college pals in a safe suburb of the Wirral. They tell me that if it's hot and wet and has three sugars, it'll be just dandy.

'Where were you at approximately nine o'clock last night?' I imagine them saying as the kettle boils. I practise not blushing and not swinging my leg, a trait that both Moll and I have picked up from Mum when we're fibbing. Dad never lies.

'Lemme see . . . nine o'clock-nine o'clock-nine o'clock . . .' Don't look up in the air for inspiration. Look 'em straight in the eye and *lie*.

'Right here, I believe, officer. Yes. I was here, attending my poorly sister.'

Maybe not bring Molly up too early on. Obvious associations between the first attack and this one. The tea's ready. Here goes.

I take the tray through, trying like fuck to think myself into the mindset of a regular boy who's slightly unsure why the police have come to see him, assumes it's to do with the deplorable attack on his sister the other night, wants to help in any way he can but doesn't see why the police haven't arrested those responsible yet. A subtle blend. I pour the tea, serve it, sit down, take a nano-sip and fix a patient smile upon the senior, and fattest, officer, who's seated directly opposite. That smile says: 'Shall we?'

Old Fatso is in no hurry. Might be hoping to string things out to a second cup. I glance to my left, where the other one is slurping his tea through his teeth in a quite disgusting manner. I catch his eye. He falters for a second and looks worriedly across at his boss, who examines his teacup rather more closely than its plain, porcelain exterior deserves, stirs his tea daintily and looks up. This is it.

'You knew Christopher Byatt?'

Hang on. What? Christopher . . . *knew*?

'I know Christy, yeah. Well, that's putting it a bit strongly, actually. You couldn't call us friends.'

'Could you call you enemies?' he says, addressing the question at the floor then looking up, eagerly, for the answer.

'No,' I reply, carefully. 'Of course not.'

'So you'd have no reason to kill him?'

He says it as though he's asking me if I'd have any reason, say, just for argument's sake, to pinch his bike. He's Harry Hypothesis, the theoretical fellow. Sorry to have to ask. All part of the job. My face must say it all. Given half a chance, my guilty conscience can take over most situations and put me firmly in the frame for crimes committed 200 miles away. Even at primary school I would blush furious scarlet when Miss Andrew announced that whoever was stealing Club biscuits from other kids' packed lunches had better stop it pronto, as she knew who the culprit was and was going to give him one last chance to stop before she took him to the police. It wasn't me, of course. I had eczema and was allergic to chocolate, as my teacher well knew, but it felt as though I was the prime suspect and everyone was looking at me and waiting for me to crack. But this time the shock of the news about Christy is too massive for me to feel anything but nothing. I'm stunned.

'He's dead?'

'You didn't know?'

'No.'

The younger but equally corpulent policeman makes a quizzical face at his superior. He nods his assent. Young Fatso clears his throat and looks a mite uncomfortable.

'Christopher Byatt was fatally injured during a dispute at The Horse And Jockey public house in Upton, round about ten o'clock last night . . .'

'Some dispute,' I interrupt.

'He was stabbed.'

'What has this got to do with me?' I suddenly say. 'I knew him, but so did lots of people.'

'Yes. Some of them mentioned your name. Can you tell us where you were last night?'

'At ten? Yes. I was here.'

I must look genuinely surprised. Old Fatso seems embarrassed. He knows I'm nothing to do with it, but he has to delve. It's his job.

'You're a difficult man to track down,' he says, trying to be jovial. Which can't be easy, if you're him. 'That, or your associates are very loyal.'

I don't know what he's talking about. It must show. He's starting to look edgy and get a bit jokey.

'Not one of them could tell me, for sure, where you live.'

He twitches his nose, still uncomfortable. Then he switches back to serious.

'So you stayed in?'

'Yes.'

'Bit boring for you, isn't it? Staying in on a Saturday night?'

Great. Right into my hands. They'll be out of here in five minutes.

'My sister was attacked on Friday night. Someone tried to rape her. Not half a mile from this very house. I've had more exciting Saturdays, yes. But there was nowhere else I wanted to be, last night. D'you know what I mean?'

He nods but persists.

'I'm sorry to be obtuse, but – you're saying that you babysat your sister? That's what you were doing last night?'

'I watched television while she rested, yes.'

'She was asleep?'

'Yes.'

'Mum and Dad?'

'The former, deceased. The latter, flat out. Fatigued from sitting up in hospital the night before, I expect.'

He bows his head. Then comes the Columbo bit. They get up and tell me that's it for now but they may need to ask me some more questions and I'm so relieved and grateful that I give them our telephone number, half-thinking we'll be out of here soon, anyway, they're welcome to it, when he turns around on the doorstep, scratching his head.

'One last thing. Last night. *Is* there anyone who can *verify* that you were in fact here? Given your two, well – *alibis* were sound asleep?'

He's smiling, but looks in pain. I actually feel quite superior, quite controlled and justly aloof.

'No. Not really. I could describe Clive Walker's missed penalty on *Match Of The Day*, if that's any good.'

He nods slowly and looks ashamed of himself again. Once they've gone I start wondering. Who the fuck killed Christy? Who put the finger on me. Tony? Baby, maybe. I wonder whether the plod will now be too embarrassed to come back and ask me about the Parkgate Hotel dust-up, having already established that I was here last night. Yep. I reckon I'm off the hook on that one. They'd have been round by now. Finally, I wonder what the heck Elvis was babbling about last night.

He seemed a bit distraught at cutting that lad, but he's

carved people up before. Of all of us, Elvis and Baby are the most callous with a blade. They just walk up and do it. I've done it twice – Stockport, home and Darlington up there when we were badly outnumbered. But it was a big deal for me. I wasn't as clinical as you need to be. It took me a couple of goes to do the Stockport boy properly. I made a bit of a mess of the job. With Elvis, he's – it's compelling to watch. The knife doesn't seem like a knife. It's like an extra part of his hand, a spare finger. It just comes out and that's that, lad on deck, bawling. There's a certainty to it which is spellbinding. You'll see him making his way across the Open End, infiltrate the away mob and you know that any second there's going to be a big gaping hole in the crowd as they dive down the terraces, terrified out of their wits, desperate to get away from him. Cause and effect.

Maybe he was just out of it. He did swill a lot of Remy in his flat while he was making the calls. And he doesn't eat. That'll be it. A combination of delayed shock from The Parkgate, drink and the cumulative effects of his depression. Plus, of course, he's bonkers. I start to think of the number of times he's talked about topping himself. I think I should call round, check he's okay. And I want to know what happened with Christy.

I change into a nondenominational combo of last-year's gear – navy, ribbed cord shoes, Lois, cable-knit crew neck and fawn Gloverall duffle coat. Very *Low*-era Bowie, and very warm when you're waiting for sporadic Sunday-service trains. I'm just leaving a note for Moll and Dad when it suddenly drops that I've hardly spoken to Moll since Friday night. Not on her own. I've been of no use to her at all. Dad, I have to allow, has been superb. He seems to understand that I'm having difficulties with all of this. All the same, though.

This is it. I've got to see this through. Fuck them! Fuck Elvis and Christy and fuck the lads that came down last night to give me a hand. It's over. It's not for me. Never was. The Pack've made that abundantly clear and they're right. I'm getting out, while I can still make the choice.

The moment the decision's made, I feel liberated. With that particular monkey off my back, it's starting to register how much of a lightweight I've been in this family since Mum died. They've been brilliant, Dad and Moll. They really have put up with some shite from me. Even now, hastening out of the front door, I can see their expressions when I declined Molly's invitation of a long walk and a pub lunch. Moll was okay, but Dad's face twitched a bit, then he did one of those over-compensating things where he's really happy and fine and relaxed and whatever you want is fine. No problem. Catch you later. I hate him for it, but really I hate me. I love them.

At least I know where they'll be. They were walking along the Wirral Way to Heswall then back again as far as The Boathouse where they were going for roast lamb and parsnips. Maybe I can redeem myself a tiny wee bit by breezing in there full of wit and good conversation and pay for the meals. I find myself getting a bit jealous about the two of them, arm in arm, so comfortable with each other. It seems as though it's always been that way. Me, fighting for attention while Mum and Dad worked every hour to build up the business, while Molly breezes in later to mop up the rewards and the affection. Maybe they don't really want me there at all. Perhaps they only asked me along out of politeness. They'll be sitting there, enjoying that uniquely gorgeous blend of lamb dripping, gravy and mint sauce, chatting intimately about Dad's plans for a new life and Moll's hopes and fears for the future and then I'll burst in.

'Hiya, Moll. Wotcha, Dad. Found that lad for you. Knocked fuck out of the cunt for you. Elvis slashed his mate. What you drinking?'

That's the sum total of my parts, now. I'm a fucking thug. I've got to find them. Him especially. I've got to – I need to change. Everything. He'll be going in three months, he'll be as gone as Mum is. I've got to find him and talk to him and, well – I want to make him love me.

'*The Sunday lamb cracks in its fat.*' I'm nervous walking down Parkgate prom. I'm not even bothered about being recognised from last night. I'm shitting myself about Molly and Dad. Am I way, way too late? What is, is, I keep telling myself. I can only do what I can do. I walk along the harbour wall like a kid, enjoying the ice-cold, ice-still air and bowl into The Boathouse, full of false-confident terror. There they are, in the corner, overlooking the Dee. They haven't seen me yet. The first look will tell me everything. The first twitch of their faces will betray how they really feel before they have the chance to set them firm in plastic smiles and pleasing salutations. Dad sees me first. He lights up. He's obviously saying, 'Look, Moll, here's our Paul,' because she turns round with a big grin, too. I hug her, then I stand, shy, in front of Dad, then I hug him, too. Briefly. Then I say: 'Thought I'd find you here!' somewhat too jauntily, and plonk myself down.

We have a good old natter. Dad's going to travel. Everywhere he always wanted to go to. He figures that he owes it to Mum to try and make himself happy. Happier. And this is his solution. He's going to go to Madagascar and Nepal and Argentina and all the places him and Mum used to pore over and dream about and know they'd never get to. I still can't help feeling a twitch of, what – hatred? Jealousy? Maybe just common 'n' garden resentment about the way everything has to be related back to her. I wish he'd do it for himself or at least just acknowledge that she's gone and she's never coming back and he'll never speak to her ever, ever again. It's wrong for him to keep telling himself they had this big, real love. She'd be married again, by now, if it'd been him that popped it.

We stroll back down the prom *en famille* and I actually feel Christmas for the first time since I was a boy. I can't figure out what it is – the coldness of the air, the woodsmoke, the peculiar light of a late-December afternoon – that triggers the associations of presents and rampant excitement and happiness and an optimism so deep and strong that it can never possibly end. I daydream about Jesus Christ while Molly and Dad rabbit about money and flats. I think I'll go to a carol service in the next few days. Me and Elvis had been talking about it. I used to love singing carols. I was never much one for the door-to-door stuff but I used to bellow them out at school. 'Ding Dong Merrily' was my favourite, especially when the choir did it and had all the intricate bits interweaving with each other. 'Kalinka' was good, as well.

'What d'you think, Paul?' asks Molly.

'Hmm?'

'Oxton? Think you could stand living with me?'

'Handy for you both. You could walk to work, son.'

Son. He called me son. I smile to myself.

'Yeah. Fab.'

I try to think what he'd like to hear more than anything else in the world. I still can't make myself tell them that I love them both.

'I'm thinking about going back to college and finishing off my A-levels. Maybe do them at Tech, or something. I know most of it, already.'

Their pleasure at this is humbling and I now know, at this moment, that I'm going to take real steps to get things back on track.

21 December 1979

Things have been going well. *Rarely well.* Family life has been almost blissful. It's how it should have been during Mum's last weeks, but there was so much fear, so much fear for *us.* This time, we're all implicitly aware that something *big* is happening. It's a landmark in our family life. Nobody really makes a special big deal about it, but I think we all understand that this is the start of the gradual break-up of the family. These are our last few weeks together. I actually went up to The Malt Shovel with Dad on Wednesday evening. I can't, I just *can't* say that I relate to him, not just like that, but he's a beautiful man. And he tried so hard to get me to down tools and come around the planet with him. I don't know.

I haven't seen or heard from Elvis. I honestly haven't really thought about him, except on Tuesday afternoon, sitting in Beatties' café eating their fine Welsh Rarebit, I started dwelling once again on all the hints he's been dropping. When I went round to his on Saturday afternoon to organise the Battle of Parkgate he was moping over Sylvia Plath again, 'Death & Co.,' 'The Fearful' and 'Ariel' itself, his very favourite suicide poems. I got him into Sylvia Plath.

Aside from the uncertainty over Elvis and the question marks over life decisions which need to be faced up to, I feel okay. Bob's back in, doing half-days and easing himself into the next twenty-two years which will take him through to retirement. He's still pretending to push me for promotion, but his fire's gone out. He really wants to tell me that if I don't get out now, I'll still be here in twenty-two years' time, having nervous breakdowns and teetering on the brink of clinical depression.

I've been passably sociable, by my own standards. I've gegged in on that whole Market Street office party scene, snogs and gropes galore, but I miss The Pack. I tried going out with Sammy, but I knew it was doomed from our first date when she started singing along to a Darts song on the jukey. Trouble is, trouble always is, I didn't actually tell her I didn't want to see her.

Worse, rather than hurt her feelings, I carried on turning up for the dates. I never was the best at finishing with girls. Usually, I just don't turn up for a few weeks and they get the picture. Little Sammy was getting more and more into me, making me cringe by telling me how she'd planned our first shag and how ace it was going to be and how she was getting me something dead special for Christmas – a cuddly puppy carrying a felt loveheart, no doubt. She tried to hold hands and link arms wherever we'd go. She even showed up in The Malt Shovel when I told her I was going out with Dad. I was going to blank her, but Dad insisted on her coming and sitting with us. Not that she said one word, other than 'lager', 'black' and 'thanks'.

Things come to somewhat of a distasteful conclusion on Thursday night. The party is at Emily's ludicrously grand house in Baskervyle Road. It's Molly's first outing since the attack and everybody's over-attentive, to the point that I know she's going to walk out, any minute.

Emily starts giving me the eye as soon as she opens the door. She must be fifteen, like Moll, maybe just sixteen, but she's a young lady. Long, straight, yellow hair, clear grey eyes and wonderful skin. Her smile is just dazzling. It's a smile I see a lot of from across the main party room, as Sammy makes a big thing of sitting with Molly and making sure she's fine. Emily tosses her mane subtly and leaves the room. I follow. My stomach flips with desire.

We're on top of her bed, kissing, my hands under her skirt, stroking her bottom through her knickers. She's got a lovely relaxed style, lying on her side with one long limb draped over my hip, rolling gently into the embrace. I move three fingers over her mound and slowly probe with my fingertips.

'It's possibly not the most appropriate time,' she whispers. It takes me a moment.

'You're on?'

She giggles and nods and looks right into my eyes, taking my middle finger and slipping it into her mouth.

'We can remove the obstacle in question.'

She drops my hand and sits bolt upright, thrilled.

'You'll do that?!'

'I'd *love* to do that!'

She gives me a sly, sidelong glance.

'Oh you bastard! Are you going to lick me?'

I push her back down onto the bed and nibble her ear.

'That's what I'm going to do. That's what you're getting.'

'You bastard,' says Emily. She gets up off the bed, eyeing me intensely while she removes her skirt and knickers, then her blouse. She slips her bra-straps off her shoulders and unhooks the back, walking towards me with smooth, shiny breasts pushed together between her arms.

'Want to?'

Do I want to. I almost eat her.

'You're beautiful. God, Emily, I'm going to fuck you.'

I kiss her neck roughly and pull her bra off, mauling her tits, kissing them and clawing them and pulling her into me. She pushes me back, breathing heavily but steady, in control.

'I want to see you.'

I strip without theatre. I've still got a good, hard body – more toned than defined – but I'm conscious of the amount I drink and I'm already aware of little rolls of fat starting to show at the top of my hips and around my lower back. I pull my boxers down a couple of inches. My dick is robustly, ruddily erect. Emily comes over, eyes glued to it and, a little clumsily I feel, trying a little too hard to be the pro, takes firm hold of it and starts to stroke her bush. She's still breathing heavily and seems tense, now. She takes my hand and places it back over her mound. I slide down, stroke her lips with two fingers then feel for the cotton ripcord. I locate it quickly and ease out the tampon. For a second I'm stumped for what to do with it, so I place it on the bedside cabinet. I imagine that that's what sends Sammy over the edge. Serves her right for spying and, worse, for not stopping things earlier.

I've been working Emily's clit for only moments, mouth clamped over her mott, arse in the air, early symptoms of lockjaw, when I feel a sharp jabbing sensation in my arsehole. Nice, I think. She's going to finger me. The pain is sporadic and nasty.

'Barthdard! Fucking cheap, filthy, dirty barthdard!'

I know that lisp. I jerk away around to find Sammy trying to ram the ejected tampon up my arse. I push her away but she flings herself on Emily and starts tearing at her hair, pulling out a fistful and going at her again. I'm about to chin her when Molly and Natasha appear from nowhere, giggling fitfully. Natasha throws a mug of water over her and they manage to calm her down and get her back downstairs. I sit there with Emily, who's very shaken. She smells wonderful. I don't want to go downstairs yet, anyway, but I wonder if it'd be pushing it to get straight back into her. Her face tells me to leave it. I think I could fall deeply, deeply in love with this Emily.

Dad's laughing over Molly's sanitised version of events. He's got a great, plummy chuckle, Dad has. You'd imagine someone like Robert Morley chuckling like this when he's not acting.

'Which only begs the question,' gasps Dad, waving his toast in the air. 'How long were you and Natasha watching?'

'Good point, Dad. Come on, Moll! How long, eh? And how was it for you?'

Molly pulls tongues and gets up to put the kettle on. How I've longed, not knowing it, for this. Why couldn't we always be like this? We weren't even like this with Mum. I instantly feel guilty for thinking it.

On the Friday, in spite of a very good offer from Molly to go to Leighton with her and Natasha, I find myself drawn to the Tranmere-Bury game. I know that I should just leave it, forget it, don't go, ever, again. I've kicked it now and it's been worth it. But I feel so strong, as a result, that I know I can handle one final trip to Prenton. I want to know what happened with Christy; and I need to see Elvis.

I work doggedly at the office until six, trying to keep my mind off it. Even Bob cried off at four. The place is deserted. I need a wank, so I beat off quickly at Sarah Mitchell's desk, thinking about Emily walking towards me with her breasts forced together. *Want to?*

I leave a note on Bob's desk that I quit at six and I'll come in a couple of days over the holiday. There's still a mountainous backlog of cases. I leave the office, shout all the best to Alfie on security and head out into the freezing foggy night. The evening is electric with the squeals of drunken girls and hopeful young men.

I bottle it at the last minute. I've done the hard part. I just need to go home, now. I could still make it to Leighton Court with Molly and Natasha. Moll'd *love* it if I came out with them, and I'd love to get off with Natasha. All I need to do is go home. So I don't walk to The Carlton. But I do catch the 10b straight to the ground. I *have* to be here. Even if I'm not part of it any more, I have to know what's going on.

I pay into the Main Stand, watch a miserable, goalless game, drink several cups of Bovril and observe The Pack keeping themselves amused in the Borough Road shed by having pogo frenzies and launching mad surges at the hoardings. Bury have brought about a hundred, but no one who wants to know. I leave twenty minutes before the end, determined that that really is it.

Saturday before Christmas is an *enormous* date in the international copping-off calendar. There are a hundred options open to me, socially, but what I end up doing – and enjoy – is a bit of shopping with Dad, a nice pint in The Ship at tea-time and a merry evening sipping sherry and planning Christmas dinner. This time last year Molly and I were dreading Christmas Day, but today there's a warmth and an intimacy between the three of us, we're a family.

She goes out with her girlfriends about nine, begs me to come, fluffs me up with stories that both Natasha and Emily are in bits over me, but no, I just want to stay in, watch football with Dad. He makes a couple of inane remarks about Dalglish always moaning at the ref. I'm quite tickled by him.

Christmas Eve, 1979

We're up early and out to Red Hill Farm for our turkey and sacks full of fresh vegetables and herbs. I do most of the heavy lifting – sacks of spuds and turnips and sprouts, but I leave Dad to go with the farmer to terminate the fowl. He drags the dripping plastic sack between his legs, trying to avoid any sort of contact with its freshly felled contents.

I'm in the kitchen, about sixish, helping Dad pluck the bird when the phone goes. Molly shouts me. It's Elvis. A wild rush of euphoria and relief. Maybe the best thing would've been to tell her to get rid of him – but I'm there in a flash. He sounds spaced out.

'Where are you, lar. I been here ages.'

'Where?'

'Thornton Hough.'

It all comes back to me. Lying in a fog of grass smoke at Elvis', what, *weeks* ago, listening to Wire and The Furs and Leonard Cohen, we decide that we're going to have a real, spiritual Christmas Eve, communing with Him through song and prayer. We are going to attend Midnight Mass. We decide that Thornton Hough, a remote and impossibly beautiful mid-Wirral farming hamlet, is to be the location for our Christmas idyll. We shall go there for Midnight Mass on Christmas Eve, come what may, we pledge.

But a lot has changed since then. I really shouldn't go. No.

'Shit. Forgot. Didn't think *you'd* turn up either. Can you hang on?'

'They won't serve me no more in that Seven Stars. Bin here

since dinner-time. I'll walk down the thingy, that hotel. Thornton Hall.'

'If they won't serve you in the Stars, they deffo won't serve you at Thornton Hall. Just wait by the green. I'll only be a minute.'

I look pleadingly at Dad. I despise myself for this. He'd love to have us all here today. But I've got to see Elvis. If I'm going to finish things off properly, I have to see him this one last time, explain how I've got to take my life somewhere else. He'll be pleased. I know he feels the same. Dad says he'll run me up to Thornton Hough, but I can make my own way home. But of course. I've never asked him for lifts, anywhere. I try to explain to him in the car that this is all about preparing the ground properly for what's going to happen in the New Year, but he's back to being silent and brooding and resigned. By the time he drops me off by the absurdly quaint sandstone bus shelter, I hate him again.

Elvis' pupils are like pinpricks and I immediately sense that he's around the halfway mark. Still, it's good to see him. He gives me a semi-embarrassed hug, not as passionate as last time, then sits back down on the bench overlooking the cricket green. The sky is phenomenal. It's late afternoon and already dark, but the December sun refuses to set, flaring streaks of red and orange through the purple-black sky. It's awesome. The two of us sit in silence, watching the oranges and reds slowly fade out of the picture. Elvis passes me a one-skinner and sparks up another for himself. He inhales deeply, leans his head back so that he's looking straight up at the sky and fires green smoke high into the air.

'Big sky,' he murmurs. I smile at this. Ever the wonder-struck existentialist, Elvis.

'What you been doing?' I ask. He thinks for a while.

'Went over there for a bit, didn't I, try to get me head together an' that, sort things out in me swede, like.'

'Where's that, like?'

'Andy and Kate's. By the park, like.'

Hang on. Kate. Smackhead Kate?

'Kate from Bebington?'

'Her. Yeah.'

He was talking to her once in Eric's. She was sat with the clique in the back room, pretending to be into Howlin' Wolf. Some of those girls in there, the ones who hang around X-Tremes, they're the sexiest, skinniest, dirtiest girls in the world – but they don't half put some shite on the jukey. Gina X followed by Howlin' Wolf followed by The Fall followed by Rockin' fucken Dopsie And His Cajun Twisters. Eclectic, argued Elvis and this Kate one. Unpardonable cack, I reasoned back. She's beautiful, Kate, but she's a phoney. I suppose the shock of being allowed into the gang has made her buy the whole deal – silly, put-on accent, guitarist-sculptor-prick boyfriend, Lark Lane flat, sluttish clothes. She was telling Elvis how ace heroin is, in that stupid, camp, drawling voice of hers. I haven't seen her around for a long time.

'She's into the other gear, isn't she?'

Elvis shrugs, but looks at the floor.

'She's into everything. Her mind's open. She's just a lovely, caring person. They're both beautiful, open people with no taboos or nothing. They never put no pressure on me an' that. Just left me to sort myself out at my own pace, lar.'

He's already talking like a Sefton Park beaut. Good. I won't miss him so much. I drag on the butt of my grass-rolly and stand up, flapping my arms against my sides. It's getting cold.

'Let's walk down The Wheatsheaf. Should be alright in there.'

Elvis reaches inside his jacket and produces a hip-flask. I take a long slug of brandy. The afterburn is delicious. Elvis stares out over the village scene. The tranquillity is unreal. The only sound comes from two excited children, pushing the round-about as fast as it will go. There hasn't been a car or a passer-by in the time we've been sitting here. He shakes his head.

'Too much, isn't it, lar?'

I nod. I feel like giving his arm a reassuring squeeze, but just can't. He stands there, motionless, not even blinking. A beautiful boy, thinking big thoughts. I don't want to get in there, with him. We start to walk.

'So what happened with Christy?'

'John Godden killed him.'

He just says it. Just says that. I feel nothing. We stare at the sky. The kids' mother calls them from one of the cottages nearby, bringing Father Christmas a tingling step closer. Wonder what *their* lives'll be like.

'Billy's had a nightmare over it. He seen it all at Halifax. Christy stabbed John when they was fighting with them subbies. Billy didn't know what to do. Didn't want to say nothing about it, but he was giving himself hell over it. Went and told Marty what he seen, like.'

Now I'm intrigued. I nod for him to continue.

'Everyone's accepted it, on the Woody, like. No one's said a word to the Busies.'

I can't help smiling at that.

'Except to put *me* in the frame, like.'

'Oh aye, they'll've given them a few jarg names. Throw them off the scent, like.'

I don't know what to say. I should take strength from their offering me up to the plod, use it as the final confirmation that I want no more of this. But it's got to me. It isn't fair. We walk slowly through the lanes, marvelling at all this rustic quiet, only a few miles from the teeming estates of Birkenhead and Liverpool. I circle round the issue.

'So, you make any big decisions, like? You gonna move in with Kate an' that?'

'Nah. Wouldn't subject them to that! No. But I don't mind their scene. Oxton's sound an' that, but we're just playing at it over here. Liverpool's a real city. One of the great cities of the world, like, and it's there, on me doorstep.'

I've been blind to how thick he really is. Like so many self-taught kids, he has a partial grasp of a whole range of goodies, artists and poets, things he thinks are cool. He learns all about them, tells you details about their lives. But he understands nothing. I can see it right now. It's tragic.

'Going to get yourself a place?'

'Dunno,' he says, nervously. 'Do *you* fancy it?'

'Me?' I'm stunned, flattered, terrified all at once. Even in this light I can see Elvis blushing.

'Don't have to say right now, like,' he laughs. I laugh too, like him, to help fill the gaps.

We have a good time in The Wheatsheaf. Intuitively we both keep it light, do a lot of reminiscing and laughing. We keep well away from any talk of flats in Sefton Park and spend the last few hours chatting away to these two very nice, very elegant middlos. Elvis, who can be brilliant in situations like this, takes the bull by the horns and starts alternatively charming them and teasing them. Regardless that they've told us their names, he insists on calling them Goldie and Dolly.

'Dolly, love, your buttons've come undone there. Just saying, like. Don't want none of these randy old farmers carting you off to the barn. You're far too classy for that. Have to be the hayloft at the very least.'

They lap it up. They're both married, their husbands are at a golf club beano and they're hinting heavily that we can come back for a nightcap.

'I hope you're both efficient workers, though,' smiles Dolly. 'We wouldn't have time to waste on apprentices.'

'Oh, we're both very thorough,' grins Elvis. 'Time-served craftsmen, the both of us.'

The middlos squeal with delight. But as quickly as Elvis solicits them, he bats them away.

'Thing is though, I'm not sure that even we, skilled and conscientious as we are, can agree to take this job on at such short notice.'

163

The good-time girls' faces drop. Elvis continues. I'm interested to hear this, too. I'd already binned the Midnight Mass for a bit of Old.

'No. Thing is, me mate here and me, we've had like a long-standing agreement that we're going to go to mass tonight. A small measure, like, towards balancing the spiritual and the material sides of our lives an' that.'

They don't look impressed. I am.

'You pair of faggots!' says Dolly, the slightly chubby one who's displaying all the décolletage. Goldie puts her hand on her wrist, to stop her.

'Whatever you want,' soothes Elvis. 'You can come with us, if you fancy . . .'

'Oh, save it. Were we just that bit too mature for you . . .?'

'You're paranoid.'

She's desperate.

'Fuck off !'

I shrug and smile. Dolly pulls her well-heeled pal to her feet and that's it. They both totter to the door, tipsy and insulted. They've got great legs. This Midnight Mass thing better be good.

We have one more pint, Guinness this time, and set off back down the lanes. Elvis is in good form, singing lustily and blessing perplexed-looking cows in the fields as we pass.

'God bless you, Ermintrude, my child. I name you Matron Saint of Dung.'

I guffaw and snitter and giggle all the way back to Thornton Hough. It's good to have him back. We clear our throats and quieten down as we step into All Saints. It's already crowded. There are no free places at the back, so we have to venture further and further down the aisle, with people turning to look at us as we pass. There's a space about halfway up, next to a smiling, rotund lady in a red hat. It'll have to do. She sort of nods and smiles as we squeeze in next to her, as if to say:

'Hello. Welcome. Nice to see the youngsters making the effort. Even if it *is* only at Christmas when you're drunk.'

The service gets going. The priest says a few words to remind us what Christmas means and then we're off and running. What a start! It's 'We Three Kings'! One of my all-time favourites. I love the 'Oh star of wonder' bit, it's ideal for my low-pitched crooning style of singing.

A style which is clearly a little too timid for the booming, heaving, exultant Mrs Redhat, who turns almost one hundred and eighty degrees to face me, rather than the altar. She belts her song out to the heavens, beaming radiantly, right into my face, singing to *me* and holding her hymn book open for me, so that I can join in too. It's too weird. She's trying to help me lose my inhibitions. She's a God slut and she's going to break me in. I can feel Elvis shuddering next to me, chewing his fist and crying with laughter. Mrs Redhat nudges me and smiles and throws her head back, a contorted torrent of joy, here to tell out her furious love. Loudly.

'OH! STAR OF ROYAL DAVID'S LIGHT! WEST-WARD LEADING STILL PROCEEDING GUIDE ME THROUGH THY PERFECT NIGHT!'

'Loada shite!' whispers Elvis, still having convulsions. He passes me the hip-flask. I take a desperate slug of brandy. Mrs Redhat is far too busy exhalting her love of God in all His magnificence to notice. She notices that I'm not singing, though, and nudges me, pointing to where we're up to in the carol. We're on the last verse. I smile and point at Elvis, who is not singing at all. I slip past Mrs Redhat, so that she's now in between Elvis and me. She dazzles him in the light of her love. She smiles and beams and shines at him. Now here's a real wretched soul to save. For the next seventy minutes I'm tortured with mirth as Elvis is slapped and jollied into embracing God by Mrs Redhat. He gives as good as he gets, singing extremely loudly, throwing his head around at the most meaningful parts, rolling his eyes and jabbering out the

165

responses to the catechism quicker than anyone else. He's thoroughly enjoying it by the end. When it's time to partake of the blood and the body of Christ he goes around twice, though I figure that this is more on account of the spicy, perfumed red communion wine than any new-found religious fervour.

Long after the last person has left the church, we're sitting in silence at the back. Elvis smokes another one-skinner. I'm too scared to join him, but wonder what Mrs Redhat looks like in the nack and whether she gets porked and whether I could do it myself.

'Will you take confession for me?' asks Elvis.

'You what?'

'Like I say, like. Certain things I have to say. Will you listen?'

''Course I will!' I blurt out, taken aback by this.

'But listen, like – like a priest does. Without judgement. Without, like, knowing it's me that's saying it. Without acting upon it.'

'You want me to listen, like – but not listen?'

'I want to say certain things. And then they're said.'

'Why not go to confession? Properly?' I offer, panicked by his sudden grave, serene expression.

'Because I want to tell *you*.'

I take a very deep breath. I know that I'm not going to like this. I try to flash him an understanding smile, and pat him on the shoulder.

'Come 'ead then, Elv. 'Course I'll listen.'

He goes into a booth. I go into the adjoining booth and pull the little velvet curtain to.

'Just talk,' I bluster. 'Whenever you're ready, like. Spew.'

For an eternity, Elvis says nothing. There's a crinkling noise as he unwraps chewing gum, or chocolate, then silence again. I'm determined that I'm not going to speak again. I'll sit here

166

all night for him, if he needs it. Thick sweet smoke filters through from Elvis' side. I hear him cough and sniffle.

'You okay, Elvis?'

'No.'

More snuffling. I hear him sucking down the heady smoke. Suddenly I go cold. I think the thought I have not been allowing myself to think since the bog-roll in his flat. Of *course* it's smack. He's the most obvious person to get into it. He'd have to be one of the first. Heroin's bang back in fashion again. And cheap. I know that much from Bob McNally. And heroin, or the idea of heroin, is such an Elvis thing. Oh, Elvis, my friend, you're such a dickhead.

'What you smoking?'

'It's the thing, lar.'

'What?'

I just want to hear him say it. But he says nothing for ages.

'He loves you, lar.'

There's silence again, then he stifles a cough. I speak quietly.

'Who does?'

I can hear him choking. I try again.

'Who does, El? You?'

Silence.

'I love you, too.'

Little cackle from Elvis.

'But he *loves* you.'

Now I see.

There doesn't seem much more that I can say. I know that, whatever I say, he's going to die. He wants to die. He's talked about it often enough. A dizzy swell of panic as I allow the thought that he's here, now, to execute a gaudy slaying of me and him both. It'd be *so* Elvis. Or how he'd like to be, at least. A suicide pact in a church in the seedling hours of Christmas morning. He's probably got a torn out page of *Ariel* in his pocket and a Joy Division tape-loop swirling around the Bang and Olufsens for the plod to find. But the seizure passes. Elvis, his voice thick with grief and lethargy, starts up a dismal plainsong:

The Burne-Jones cartoons
Have preserved her eyes
Still, at The Tate, they teach
Cophetua to rhapsodize.

'Stop it, El,' I plead. His voice is frightening.

Thin like brook-water
With a vacant gaze
The English Rubaiyat was still-born in those days

The thin, clear gaze the same
Still darts out faunlike from the half-ruined face
Questing and passive . . .
Ah, poor Elways case . . .

He breaks off. I hear him gulping and snuffling. What a waste.

I can just about hear it in his voice as he tries to crank himself up a gear.

'You going to Crewe?'

'Doubt it.'

'Why?'

'I'm jibbing all that.'

'I am. So how about it? One last awayday?'

'Dunno.'

A mad, elongated, silent sobbing noise from Elvis, then a dribbling sniff.

'I'm never going to see you again, am I?'

He may be right.

'Don't talk soft.'

I sit there for a while before I twig that Elvis has gone.

When I get outside the church, there is nothing to see, nothing to hear. Just his smell, his sweet, wasted smell. Walking home, I feel better about myself. It's exactly the same as the one other time in my life that I walked down these lanes. The night when it was told to me that Mum would die for sure of cancer. I felt separated from humanity that night, different from everyone else. It felt like I was walking away from Mum's suffering and into a whole new world of private, personal sorrow. I felt powerful for it. And tonight, also, it feels as though I'm walking away from something, leaving it forever and heading into something bigger. I don't know what. But it'll be okay, because for perhaps the first time I know that it'll be something good. My life is not horrible. There's something here for me.

28 December 1979

I'm glad to be tucked away in the office where I can keep myself occupied with the mundanities. Bob's left a note from yesterday saying he'll be in at twelve. Yesterday was such a bluey for me. Over Christmas and Boxing Day, the Fabulous Drinking Carty Family broke new records for insobriety. Even Dad was reduced to mumbling fool status by mid-Boxing Day, got at from the moment of her arrival by Aunty Geraldine, Mum's famously tipsy older sister and the one member of her clan to remain in contact.

Instead of bunging us fivers or record-tokens at Christmas-time and birthdays, Aunty Ged always sends Molly and I these fantastically self-righteous Patience Strong cards, always featuring a bunch of flowers and a stanza of third-form verse on the subject of strength through prayer and friendship. The highlight of these cards is the scrawled message from Aunt Ged herself, mendaciously asserting that, instead of a present this year, last year, every year, she was giving a donation *in our name* to the Martyred Sisters Of Assumpta Lourdes Minibus appeal or the Joey Doonan Kidney Appeal. Was she fuck. She was pissing our present up the walls of The Newington Arms off Bold Street.

As we've got older and more perverse, Aunty Ged's card has become the most anticipated highlight of whatever momentous occasion Moll and I are celebrating. All other missives are chucked to one side as we locate and tear open the tell-tale mauve envelope and read the verse aloud, tears of mirth usually preventing us from completing the ritual oration.

This year, her parsimony could have been her undoing.

Instead of splashing out on a postage stamp and giving us the singular pleasure of receiving her outlandish fibbery by mail, she decided to cut back on expenses and hand us her card over the dinner table. This is to wave a stick in the face of providence. Sloshed out of our senses with hair o' th' dog Bloody Marys followed by a then-essential trip to The Old Quay, Molly and I beg like schoolkids who know the answer, to be the one chosen to receive the card. Just the one between us this year because we're as good as grown-up. Dad hides in the kitchen, pretending to perfect his gravy as Moll and I bring Aunty Ged extra cushions and refill her sherry glass, *pleading* with her to let us read out this year's message. Seeing as I'm a lad and Aunty Geraldine is a boozy old strumpet, I get the card. Molly's already cracking up as I ceremoniously rip open the envelope with a knife and read out the sickeningly optimistic passage on the card. I manage to pull a sincere face that suggests the words mean a lot to Moll and me. Molly disappears under the table, quaking and heaving, ready to explode with giggles. Dad keeps himself busy in the kitchen. I catch a stifled snigger from him and nearly blow, myself. I steady myself, a remarkable feat of self-restraint, ready to announce this season's excuse for not giving us kids a Chrimbo prezzie.

My Dears, I am still so heartbroken over the cruel taking of our beloved, immaculate Patsy. I know that you will appreciate it that, this Christmas, rather than something you might not like, I have made a donation in your names to the Nancy Corrigan Lung Cancer Appeal.
God Bless The Both Of You
Your Loving Aunt
Geraldine

I look up from the card and smile wonkily at her. 'Bollocks!' I declare.

She looks at me, stunned, clueless. I hear loud, fruity chuckling from the kitchen and relentless peals of painful giggling from under the table. After a full minute of crying, shrieking hysterics, Molly's hands appear on the table-top, then her reddened face is dragged into view, tearstained and utterly helpless with laughter. Then Aunty Ged starts as well. She's a handsome, bosomy woman and her laugh matches superbly. Dad comes into the room, his eyes wet, and the four of us piss ourselves for ages.

'You bloody shower of bastards,' says Ged, eventually. We have to carry drink to her all day in reparation for our deplorable rudeness. We dispose of *all* the wine and spirits in the house, which is a substantial amount, including a deep, fragrant bottle of Nuits St George which Dad later tells us was worth money. We hobble down to The Old Quay at seven o'clock and don't return until nearly midnight, at which point I collapse in the act of mixing them Pernod-and-bleach fresh-breath elixir.

Next day my head is banging like never before. I sit up, dizzy and nauseous. All sorts of mad snippets of voices and talk are flitting in and out of my dim consciousness.

'*We're the Rubaiyat, aren't we.*'

Not a question.

Poor fucking Elvis. A gilded youth in every sense except reality. In reality he's had it. *Yeux Glacques*. But this is what he wants, surely. Everything about Elvis aspires to this wanton, bored self-degradation. He applies the same whims and fashions to his life as he does to his other fashion statements. He doesn't think for a second that he's in love with me. He's playing out a role which he's written for himself and which was written for him many years ago and many times again, since. The Thin White Duke. The Wasted Youth. Poor cunt.

'*One last Awayday.*'

I stuff my pillow over my head and try and stop the ringing, the high-pitch, monotone ringing and the voices. One last Awayday? What for? For whom?

I get myself up and I get myself dressed and I just feel *bad*. It's only just gone eleven. Those bastards'll sleep until tea-time. I have a gingerish stab at cleaning up the mess, but I find myself stopping halfway through the most rudimentary task, forgetting why I have an empty bottle of Hunt's tonic in my hand and where I'm supposed to be going with it. I go back to my room. More voices.

'*But he* loves *you.*'

Shit. I try to sort out my presents. Lots of Clinique stuff and books and records from Molly, and a beautiful sky blue cashmere V-neck Dad's brought me from Westaway & Westaway in London. He thought the colour might not be me, but I love it. I hold it to my face, feeling the luxury.

I stack my new albums on top of the record pile and start flipping through my collection. I stick on 'Frankie Teardrop' by Suicide. I make a real effort, humming and pacing about, not to think about Elvis. I feel more and more listless. I should force myself out, do something, go to work, even. But instead I play 'Spanish Stroll' by Mink Deville and 'Song For Europe' by Roxy and start to feel very significant.

Bob comes in shortly after twelve. He looks much better, these days. Bob, who for all his anti-establishment rhetoric, would never have defrauded his paymasters in the past, shuffles a few papers, pulls a few impatient faces and stands up, exasperated. He fishes an obviously new and somewhat oversized Little-woods car-coat off the back of his chair.

'Come 'ead. Enduv de yeer. Out wid dee old. In wid de new. Plus ça change, Paul lad. Plus ça change.'

The Copperfield this afternoon is mercifully free of Christmas throngs. I never thought I'd ever see its tatty carpeting again. Bob asks for a pint of water, much to Raymond's displeasure, so I over-compensate with a large

Bloody Mary and a glass of Guinness. We perch on our usual stools at our usual table.

'Take it you seen all dee aggro at Tranmere?'

'Nope,' I say, almost smugly. 'Never went.'

'Oh . . .'

It's almost a question. I can well comprehend his surprise. At about the time I was reading out Aunty Ged's Christmas humbug on Boxing Day, Tranmere and Chester were warming up before kick-off at Prenton and The Pack were launching a pincer-movement on the thousand-plus Chester turnout in the Open End. It's been all over the *Echo* and *The Daily Post*, but most significant was a line in *The Express* which notes that supporters of Tranmere Rovers were '*again*' involved in trouble, before, during and after their Boxing Day fixture with local rivals Chester. It's a game I would not have contemplated missing for anything. But I missed it. I even forgot to ask what the score was until half-past nine in the pub.

I'd be satisfied that I'd rid myself, for good, of this thing if I hadn't thrilled so much at the reports of ag in the newspapers, and cut out snippings from each horrified eye-witness account.

'How come, like?'

'I'm done with it, Bob, mate. New Year's resolution. I'm thinking of going back to college to finish off my A-levels.'

Brief, shocked silence from Bob. I half-fear he's about to get resentful on me, when his face splits into the most amazing, glorious beamer. He has tears in his eyes and he's biting his lower lip. He puts a hand on my shoulder and eyes me *respectfully*.

'Dass byoodifull, Paul, lad. I'm made up for yeah. I'm fucken made up.'

He gives my shoulder a rough shake, looks at his pint of water and marches over to the bar. He's back moments later carrying two wine glasses. Raymond follows in his wake with a bottle of red wine.

'Sorry, lad. No bubbly. But diss gear'll do for toasting. Come 'ead, Ray, get yeah-self a glass, lad. Chop-chop!'

Raymond obediently returns with another wine glass and a couple of large Jamies, on the house. By half-two we're gassed and Bob is talking such complete cack that it's probably The Truth. Two wine bottles stand empty and a third is about to be drained as Bob pours and waves his free hand around:

'See, yeah time has come, Paul, lad. Yeah time of questioning. The time when yerrask . . . Why? Why's it gorra be *diss* way? How's about if I wanna do *dah*? Norrevree one asks diss question. Most don't. But dose oo doo . . .'

He breaks off to make a mystical, comically knowing, nodding face. His eyeballs go huge and white and bolly. His sharp little teeth glisten with saliva.

'. . . *DEY* are de ones oo av taken a lewk troo de window on de werld!'

He looks me right in the eye. He's nodding fervently, now, religiously.

'Juss like Marco Polo, juss like Samuel Goldwyn, whoever – juss like fucken Hittleh if yeah want – *yew* are *now* taken a lewk troo de werld's window an' yer asken yeah self . . .'

He beats his chest in a ridiculous manner.

'. . . where's *my* bit!? Which way shall . . . *I* go!?'

I stifle a very real need to laugh out loud and manage instead to nod solemnly. Embarrassed by the way Bob is staring so meaningfully at me, panting, I pick up the empty wine bottle and crane round to Ray at the bar, signalling for another. Ray, too, is nodding solemnly. I am surrounded by men of a certain age whose chance to take a peek through the world's window and choose their acme Life Plan has passed them by. I feel tremendously fond of them both – and terrifically depressed.

Ray brings over another bottle of wine and tells us it's his last in stock. He can shoot down to the Cash and Carry if we're going to be needing more. We decline. I decide that it can't do any harm for Bob to know the full extent of my interest in Tranmere. Just talking about the Chester riot has got me palpitating and right now, it all seems far from final. I try to explain to him that I can't put a lid on all this – Elvis, The Pack, the code – without feeling that it *is* actually *over*, that I'm through with it.

'Is it finishable?'

'Yes.'

'By you?'

I look him in the eye then look away.

'Don't know.'

'No. Tort not.'

He knocks back his wine and half-examines his glass, as if a drop more might be concealing itself somewhere. He squints at me.

'Don't be a prick, Paul. Yev done de 'ard part. De 'ard part is *seeing*. Just stay away, now.'

'Dunno, Bob.'

I think hard about what I can offer to help him understand.

'I like it.'

Red anger flashes across his face.

'Typical, fucken petit bourgeois, self-despising Catholic! You want *dem* to fuck yeroff, don't yeah? Yeah can't do it yeah self!'

He's right. This odd little fellow with high principles, sharp features, shite hair and little experience of life, of living, has put the whole thing into clear focus. It can't be me who does the leaving. I can't rationalise it any more than I can ignore it. It's just there. A virus. A need. It can only be voided by them. The Kingmakers.

Bob leans forward and grasps my wrist.

'Don't go back, lad!'

'No.'

'I mean it!'

'I won't.'

Bob smiles thinly, unsure, burps and gets up for the toilet.

Batesy's brother, Big Batesy comes in, carrying a giant holdall. Big Batesy is known to one and all as a kite who goes to France, Belgium, Holland, Germany and comes back with splendid merchandise – Adidas, Puma, Patrick – this sort of thing. He's got a pile of Campri Stanley jackets, mumbles something about the Lake District, good gear, the real thing, and asks for a tenner. I've seen a few of these around Liverpool. I pick out a nice navy blue one. Go nicely with my cashmere jumper and the Donnay strapovers I've seen in Sportsworld, Heswall. Looks like I'm going to Crewe, then.

30 December 1979

When Peel played 'Another Girl, Another Planet' on The Festive Fifty last night, that made my mind up. A farewell to Elvis. A farewell to The Pack. This trip to Crewe is a farewell to all of that.

But none of them are here. I've walked the length of the 12.10 London train and there's not a soul I know. The train is mobbed to bursting point with hyped-up urchins, over-talking, lighting ciggies, hanging out the windows and blowing fringes out of their eyes self-consciously. I only recognise a handful of them. This scally thing has gone overground. They're everywhere, every one of them wearing ski-jumpers, jumbos, blue Kios and Luhta bubble jackets or Stanleys. Even Bury had about half a dozen the other night, defiantly standing apart from the rest of the wools in their mob. There must be close on three hundred here – a First Division-sized crew.

Just as the train's pulling out, a breathless Danny Allen comes haring along the platform. He just about gets on board the first carriage. I make my way back down the train to find out what's up. He's skittish, but seems pleased to see me.

'Kin'ell, Paul, lar! Where you been? I heard you was on the run!'

I laugh, quite pleased by the rumour. It's not like they've been saying I was caught in bogs at Birkenhead Park, or something.

'No! I've just, like – I've been a bit out of things.'

He looks like he wants to be convinced.

'Just get off for a bit, like?'

'Something like that. Yeah.'

He catches his breath. He's still nervous. He's not his usual gushing self.

'Spoke to Marty?'

'No. Why?'

He doesn't pursue it. I can see that he'd rather not be talking to me. This is starting to feel like a mistake. I'll go to Crewe, watch the game, fuck off. That's it.

'Where's Elvis?'

'Haven't seen him, like. You seen him?'

'No, mate. Haven't seen him for a while. Haven't seen either of yez since we done them ponces in Parkgate.'

'Ta for that. Appreciated it. I've had to keep me head down since then,' I lie.

It's obvious Danny wants to believe me. There's an uncomfortable silence, broken by me.

'Where's all the boys, anyway? Who's all this crew?'

Danny slaps his forehead with the palm of his hand.

'Shit! The burial!'

He explains how Christy's body had to be held over Christmas while the police continued their inquiries. The funeral was taking place at eleven o'clock this morning.

'Shit! They'll murder me!'

'It's not the end of the world.'

Danny pauses and grins.

'It is for him!'

We both find this terrifically amusing and are still chuckling when the train pulls in at Runcorn. A delirious shout goes up. Two full-on Mods are standing on the opposite platform, waiting for the Liverpool train. One of them has a distinctly un-Modish moustache and hateful, angry black eyes. The whole train's laughing and whistling at them and singing 'We Are The Mods'. For some reason they think we're Everton.

''Ello! 'Ello! Blue and white shite!' chant the redoubtable Mods.

A deafening chorus of 'Don't Be Mistaken' is volleyed back.

Fuck knows how all this lot know the words. They've never been to Tranmere, most of them.

'Dzuh Road End!' shout the Runcorn Red Army, sounding more impenetrably Scouse than the most gummy-faced Vauxhall Road stevedore. Tranmere resort to 'You're Gonna Get Your Fucken Heads Kicked In' and pretend to steam off the train, resulting in the happy spectacle of the two Mods vaulting the mesh fence in one bound and running like fuck. They only stop when the bray of laughter catches up with them and cuts through their fear. Muzzy Man gives it two fingers while his mate bows and touches his forelock, winning friends.

We reach Crewe in no time at all and, regardless of the almighty mob streaming up the steps and out of the station and into the distance, I've still got the butterflies. I don't know this firm and I don't want to get too attached to them. Danny's lightened up sufficiently to screw himself to my shoulder.

The police are caught completely unawares. The four of them in the station run after the mob in a ridiculous Keystone Cops parody, helmets off and tucked under their arms shouting:

'Get back in fouckin stirshen! You're meant to be on next train!'

From this, we surmise that their cunning intelligence network has been tipped off that The Pack are somewhere between here and Merseyside and decide to give it half an hour to see if they show. The sideshow with the Busies keeps us entertained. Hundreds of Tranmere New Boys are swarming down the bridge towards Crewe's ground, running over car roofs and kicking in shop windows as mob fever sets in. Traffic's at a standstill. One bloated, red-faced copper, the very definition of the old-fashioned Bobby, struggles to keep up and eventually throws the towel in. He comes gasping back up the bridge, helmet askew. Danny and me are in pleats with him. This must be the last straw. He goes bonkers:

'YOU TWO! STOP SMIRKING!'

This only has the effect of making us giggle stupidly.

'THUGS! SCUM! YOBBOES! YOU'RE BIGGEST SHOWER GOING, TRANMERE!'

'I say officer, steady on!' I offer.

'Look like you could do with laying off the Chrimbo Pubbing for a few days, matey,' adds Danny. This isn't helpful. The purple-faced copper hits the Captain Hurricane raging fury button. He pulls the helmet off his beefy head and hurls it at us, following up with an attempted human battering ram, head down, charging us like a wild bull. He actually shouts 'Aaaargh!' as he runs. There's no choice but to step to one side and let him fly pell-mell into the door of the Red Star office. Danny, helpless with laughter, picks up the helmet and sticks it on his own skinny bonce.

'Come 'ead!' he gasps. 'Let's do one! We'll find the others!'

Indeed we do. We've barely ordered our drinks in the lounge bar of The Royal Hotel, Crewe's pub, when forty or fifty of them, all wearing dark suits or jackets, stream in. They look fantastic. They look wild. There's no Elvis. Marty, who's a bit shifty and doesn't make proper eye contact, explains that they've come straight from the cemetery in a removal van. Nice intelligence, coppers.

Eddie's out and there's clearly been something of a wake-cum-party. It's too weird that Godden, the psycho, has been to the funeral of the man he killed. I'm not surprised he's had a few drinks. Only Marty looks stable. Baby comes up to the bar and looks right through me. Looking around the place, indeed, it's clear that I'm being dealt a wide one. I decide that I've got nothing to lose.

'Am I meant to have done something, Mart?'

'What yer on about?'

'Youse. All of you giving us the cold shoulder.'

Marty laughs and looks embarrassed, but still doesn't look me in the eye.

'You're going para, mate.'

'I don't think so, mate. Look at this cunt!'

I jerk my thumb at Baby. Now Marty really does laugh.

'Him! He wouldn't recognise his own dick at the moment.
Hardy spiked the punch with acid. All hands are wilden on it!'

I'm nowhere near satisfied with this – there's definitely
something been said – but Danny is tickling them all with his
account of the athletic copper and it seems wrong to heavy the
atmos. I'm irritated at how quickly a no-mark like Danny has
become accepted, but it's just the way their squiffy order of
things works. He's living on the Noctorum, smack in between
the Ford and the Woodchurch. He's bumping into people all
the time. He's known, he's a face and that's that. I have cause
to be grateful to him, anyway, when he and Batesy take me to
one side.

'It's just that . . . some of them got told that you was
slagging Tranmere down.'

'Who?'

'Ah, some knobheads. Mates of The Nosh Queens.'

I do a quick scan back over everything I've said to Jackie
and Sonia. I suppose it's true. I've said a few disloyal things.
Batesy joins in.

'Way in The Copperfield told our Wobbie you was jibbin'
Twanmere for good. Said you was in there yistadee.'

'I was. And I'm here, aren't I?'

They look a bit embarrassed.

'Look. There's been a lot of talk, specially after Parkgate,
and then you never showed for Bury,' says Danny. 'Some of
them've got you down as a snide Odge, like. People get mad
ideas.'

This is so outrageous that I laugh out loud. Batesy looks
heartbroken.

'Look. I like you, like. You're or-white. You get stuck in
and you're or-white. Some of these no-marks don't know

what duh-won about. It's good that you've come today, like. It puts an end to the woomers.'

'Unless you're spying for the Odge, like,' laughs Danny.

'Fuckenell, Dan. Coulda said something, like. We've had the whole train ride and you never said nothing about this.'

He blushes and holds his hands up, accepting the criticism, but I can't warm to him. He's a Scouser, and here he is going on about Odgies. I'd respect him more if he just didn't say anything. How I wish I hadn't come.

But one by one, as the drink flows and the acid starts to wear off, they start coming over, shaking my hand. The extent of the rumour is confirmed by the number of boys who say, inadvertently, 'Good to have you back.' When Marty comes over and tells me, 'You can't leave,' I take it as a compliment. There's only one thing for it. I've got to get as drunk as they are. For all that I feel weird, I'm being made welcome and everyone is having a brilliant time.

The good humour continues as the Legends stagger in, wearing an extraordinary array of ladies' hats which they've pinched from Brown's, having come the Chester route. Silence is called for as Danny runs through his story again, and everyone jumps to their feet for the chorus of:

'THUGS! SCUM! YOBBOES! YOU'RE BIGGEST SHOWER GOING, TRANMERE!'

I take a quick tour of their faces, gloriously plastered, and can't help loving them. Eddie, completely gone, is wandering around with his best kecks rolled up to his knees and a knotted handkerchief on his head. It's queer to square him as a Fascist mastermind, this toothless, gurning fool. Elvis' theory on the sudden rise of the National Front among young males was that they've got a good logo and the girl on the leaflets is gorgeous. Ah, Elvis. What you up to, matey? Some last ride, this.

Billy Powell, grinning inanely, hands me a pint and plonks himself down next to me. I'm inexplicably chuffed.

'How yuh been, kidder?' he asks.

'Sound.' Pause. 'Thanks for that, the other night.'

He inclines his head, robotically, eyes bugged-out, voice staccato.

'So how yuh been, kidder?'

It's going to be a long afternoon.

The jukey is cranked up on full and there's much energetic skanking to The Specials and frenzied kick-dancing to 'Teenage Kicks' and 'Eton Rifles', both of which are played repeatedly. The landlord has got over his initial timidity and is making a fortune on turkey butties and the bizarre cocktails everyone is inventing for each other. Trying to get involved, I've invented The Merton Parka for Batesy, comprising vodka, Pernod and blackcurrant cordial. Everyone participating has to drink it in one shot before moving onto the next dedication. Baby proposes The Gay Blade for me, whose ingredients, Babycham, Martini and lemonade he shouts out in a silly camp voice. 'Gay' is a piss-take some of the lads've started using for benders. I don't think even Baby thinks I'm queer after the way his sister's been chasing me. But he, of all of them, has never liked the fact that I'm not from Downtown or one of the estates. I'm not a Brother. He doesn't know me. To Baby I'm a 'puff', a 'ponce', someone who isn't as thick as him, doesn't talk the same as him – hence the stupid fucking voice when he orders. Some of the heads laugh nastily and clock me with sly kites to see how I'll react. I should knock the little cunt out.

No. I should just do one now, go the bogs and never come back again, but something compels me to stay.

A couple of young rips are in there with their mums. As they get more and more drunk they start dancing and flirting with us. Godden, bladdered, persuades one of the hags that Eddie hasn't had a shag in six months. This woman looks about sixty and is clearly delighted at the prospect of getting humped by anyone, let alone a sex-starved desperado. Her shiny red face cracks into a thousand lines as she clutches John's hand, rasping at the vulgarity of it.

'You cheeky Scouse get! That's no way to get round a lady!'

A brisk whip-round realises £11.37 and, emboldened by another barley wine and coaxed on by her daughter and her chums, she goes into the snug with Eddie and sucks him off in full view of our jostling, cheering mob. Eddie's face is a picture as he sprecks up, a brain-frazzled Vietnam vet just sitting back, watching the pretty bombs go off. Again, as I have so many times during the past couple of years, I want the lads to know that I'm alright, I can be relied upon, I'm one of them, even if I do come from the suburbs. I'd do anything for them.

A paving slab crashes through the lounge window, landing at the very spot where, five minutes ago and any second now Marty would have been sitting. He looks properly jolted. The effect on The Pack is devastating. Without conference we leave by the side door, so most of us are out of the pub and running at Crewe before they get a chance to hit us with the bricks and bottles they've stockpiled on the other side of the road.

There's a tidy firm of them but they're on their toes the second they see us. It's not the big scatter, more of a gradual retreat accompanied by much jumping up and down and come-and-have-a-go gestures. There's bound to be more of them down the road, but we still leg after them, peppering their Harrington-jacketed backs with pint-pots.

We get round the corner into Gresty Road itself and it's straight into the eye of the storm. They come at us from everywhere, hitting us with halfies, traffic cones, bits of scaffolding, the lot, and follow through by running right into us, really having a go. It's the first time I've seen us back off in ages. Casey, looking absurd in a pink pill-box hat, gets smashed on the head with a length of steel tubing. He's down and out. I'm shitting it, here. There's about seventy of us, all good heads, but Crewe have got more. Leading them from the front is a big, mangy Rasta in a black tea-cosy hat who's straight into us, kicking out athletically and, thankfully, missing. This often happens. A big cunt'll dive in first and try and take the whole crew of us but once he's thrown a few haymakers and tired himself out, Billy and some of the other little hyenas'll jump him from both sides, pull him down and fill him in, good style. Billy obviously doesn't fancy this Rasta. No one can get near him with his fucking Grasshopper routine. He's not exactly damaging us, but he's giving Crewe confidence. I've never seen them up for it like this. We've steadied ourselves at the end of the road, but Crewe are having a real knock.

I'm up against the door of a little terraced house, giving it to some dirty-faced subbie who looks like Benny out of *Crossroads*. Hardy and Eddie are tearing at the boarded-up window of the next house, prising planks of wood out. They run back into the street, screaming.

'Get the nigger! Get the fucken nigger!'

They lay into him, slapping him round the head and shoulders with their bats. Still he stands. I snot Benny three or four times and let him go down. The Rasta has just slammed Eddie to the floor with his forearm and is now kicking and sweeping at a paralysed Hardy. I kick him in the small of his back and hear him shout out in pain. He turns, pressing his back with one hand. Why am I doing this? For Hardy and fucking Eddie? He throws a punch which I manage to duck, just getting a flick in on his balls. He winces, crouching down to get his breath. Marty comes dancing over and jumps in, two-footed into his chest, sending him ricocheting into a house wall. He's on his own now, surrounded, but still he stands, yellow eyes staring and crazy as he faces up to us.

There's a roar and the hum of the mass-flapping of wide trousers as Crewe come screaming back up the street. Behind them, legging them, are the New Boys, loads of them, panicking the wools into a chaotic stampede. It's pandemonium. Crewe's rearguard are getting pulled back and hopped on, while the rest of them carry on running. Some of them are really young and their fear is plain to see. The Rasta stands heroically in the middle of the fleeing tide, delaying the soon-come pasting. I catch him with a scorcher, probably the best punch I've thrown. He's stunned by the force of it and I allow myself a quick glance back at Marty. Whatever Elvis has told him, maybe the boys can now see for themselves that I'm no dickhead.

The rasta hobbles backwards and this time it's the end. Hardy, Marty and Baby all run into him at once, leathering him horribly, leaving him on the deck spewing bile. Most of Crewe's mob has got away now, but a couple try to drag their battered leader away.

'These avven'ad it!' shouts Baby Millan.

Damien, Tony and Billy bounce over and start getting into them, as well. I'm rooted to the spot. They're murdering them. It's horrible. Baby strolls back over, hand inside his pocket. One glance around to make sure then he's bending over them, arm jerking up and down like he's trying to start a lawnmower. Their screaming and howling is hideous.

He saunters back with the other three rats, pulling his shirt out to wipe the blade. I'm still standing here. He gives me a half-smile and then, in slow motion, as he draws level with me, the hand's out of his pocket again and he's flicking at my face.

'Ponce.'

There's no real pain. It just feels like a sharp punch, right on the cheekbone. I put my hand to the spot, stunned. I can hear laughter, manic, disembodied laughter, and I turn, slowly, to see them lolloping away. The last I see of them, ever, is Baby Millan turning round and grinning at me, running his finger down his face.

'You can't leave.'

Not a plea. A statement of fact.

I feel sick. I retch, but nothing comes out. The blood's flowing freely. I'm trying to think clear, talk myself through this. I really don't want to go to hospital in Crewe. I should try to get home and go from there. I could lose a bit of blood in that time. Maybe I could get to Chester. Can't be more than twenty minutes on the train. Yeah. Chester. That's where I'm heading.

Gresty Road, scene of chaos as recently as five minutes ago, is deserted except for a few latecomers scurrying to the ground. One old boy gives me an anxious look, seems as though he's going to come over, then thinks better of it, stares right ahead and lengthens his stride. I get to the end of the street. It seems to take ages. Then I turn right and head for the station. Out of here. Out of this.